DRAW DOWN THE LIGHTNING

Carter O'Brien was greased lightning with a gun, the best freelance fighting man in the business. That's why the greenhorn wanted to hire him. The trouble was, he had been sworn to secrecy about his own mysterious mission. Someone else knew about it though: two attempts had already been made on the greenhorn's life. O'Brien decided to tag along for a while, little knowing that he would soon face his toughest challenge . . . and get the surprise of his life.

Books by Ben Bridges
in the Linford Western Library:

MARKED FOR DEATH
HELL FOR LEATHER
MEAN AS HELL

T. MILBURN

5/16

DATE DUE FOR RETURN

1 7 JUN 2016

4 - OCT 2016

- 9 AUG 2019

BEN BRIDGES

DRAW DOWN THE LIGHTNING

Complete and Unabridged

LINFORD
Leicester

First published in Great Britain in 2007 by
Robert Hale Limited
London

First Linford Edition
published 2008
by arrangement with
Robert Hale Limited
London

British Library CIP Data

Bridges, Ben, *1958* –
   Draw down the lightning.—
   Large print ed.—
   Linford western library
   1. Western stories
   2. Large type books
   I. Title
   823.9′14 [F]

   ISBN 978–1–84782–316–8

Published by
F. A. Thorpe (Publishing)
Anstey, Leicestershire

Set by Words & Graphics Ltd.
Anstey, Leicestershire
Printed and bound in Great Britain by
T. J. International Ltd., Padstow, Cornwall

This book is printed on acid-free paper

For Link Hullar
The best of men,
and the best of friends

1

The last thing O'Brien expected to do that day was kill a man — but that's the way it panned out.

It happened one blustery afternoon in the spring of 1887. O'Brien had just spent a hard day in the saddle, coming down out of a maze of narrow valleys and wind-scoured gulches to the north and east, the sun just beginning a slow descent toward the granite peaks away to his right.

Beneath him, his stocking-legged blood-bay horse had been picking a cautious path down through groves of close-growing piñon pine and golden aspen since noon, and now, man and mount alike were finally beginning to feel the effects of their long, arduous trek.

It had taken them the better part of a week to cross these southern Rockies, during which time O'Brien had grown as heartily sick of his own company as he had of his own lousy cooking. But the bulk of the journey was behind him at last, and if everything he'd heard was true, then he expected to find fresh challenges up ahead — or more accurately, down below — in a mining town not twenty miles distant, by the name of Skeeter Creek.

A gust of wind tore at them as they descended a grassy slope between shelving belts of lodgepole pine. It tugged at the rolled brim of O'Brien's tobacco-brown Stetson and shoved him sideways in his battered Texas double-rig, providing a chilly reminder of the winter just gone that made him tuck his whiskery jaw even deeper into the collar of his buttoned wolfskin jacket and think longingly about the hot, strong coffee he'd be cooking up at day's end.

Man and horse continued to drop lower into rugged foothills until, at length, they came to a stage-coach trail. It wasn't much more than a ribbon of hard-packed dirt that cut down through a timbered incline spattered with marsh grass and strawberry leaves, but it was the first sign of civilization O'Brien had seen in damn'-near seven whole —

Before he could finish the thought, his attention was taken by two horsemen a couple hundred yards below him, who were blocking the trail ahead of a black, piano-box buggy.

Two horsemen with guns in their fists and bandannas tied across their lower faces.

Quickly, before they could spot him, he turned the blood-bay back off the trail and into some tall, twisted sagebrush, then got the animal turned around again so that he could take a closer look at what was happening below from the cover of its brittle-looking evergreen branches.

Working by touch, he unbuckled one saddle-bag and drew out an old but serviceable pair of field-glasses, which he then brought up to his narrowed, pale-blue eyes.

The buggy, he saw, had one occupant: a man in a loose, tan-coloured topcoat and a light, narrow-brimmed hat, whose gloved hands — one of which was still clutching the reins of his stalled two-horse team — were now raised shoulder-high. Even from this distance the poor sonofabuck had the stiff, awkward look of a greenhorn about him ... but then, O'Brien guessed, he had every right to look stiff and awkward with a gun stuck in his face.

The men who were in the process of robbing him, by contrast — for the guns and bandannas told their own story — appeared altogether tougher and more trail-wise. The first, a thin man of what appeared to be average height, was wearing a high-crowned black hat drawn low over shaggy, corn-yellow hair, and buckskin gauntlets pulled up over the cuffs of a black pea-coat. Evidently he was the spokesman of the pair, because he was doing all the talking.

His silent partner, meanwhile, was content just to sit a chestnut mare slantwise across the trail about four, five yards behind him, and treat their victim to a menacing glare as he flexed thick fingers around the grips of a Remington Army .44. At this distance, and in the red, uncertain light of approaching sunset, O'Brien could only get an impression of him: that he was a tall, intimidating bear of a man in a dark, wide-brimmed hat and bright yellow mackinaw.

Then the first road agent was speaking again — snarling, more like — and making angry little gestures with his own Cavalry Colt to help get his message across. When he was finished, he kicked his spotted pony up alongside the buggy and brought the long-barrelled .44/.40 around in a hard, driving sweep that caught the green-horn square in the face and flung him sideways across the wagon-seat.

Flinching at the brutality of it, O'Brien decided that he'd seen enough

— *more* than enough — and without taking his eyes off the men below, stuffed the field-glasses away and flipped the restraining thong off the hammer of the gun he wore at his right hip.

At the sound of his bellowed, '*Yee-haah!*', the blood-bay leapt back out onto the trail, its earlier fatigue now forgotten, and at about the same time, the gun — a .38-calibre Colt Lightning — seemed almost to leap into its rider's palm, spilling the orange glow of sundown off its short barrel as he brought it up and triggered a shot skyward.

'*Hey, down there!*'

The gunblast shattered the thin, high country silence and threw a scare the size of Arkansas into Pistol-whipper and his buddy, and for a fistful of seconds after that there was only chaos as the startled robbers fought to bring their equally spooked horses back under control.

Thundering on towards them, O'Brien

fired the Lightning again, right over the robbers' heads this time, just to let them know that he meant business, and that they should sink spurs and make dust while they still could.

At that, their faces whipped up and around in his direction, and above creased bandannas sucked in and blown out again by their rapid, flustered breathing, he saw their furious eyes fix on him, and knew that this was the moment when they either ran — as he hoped they would — or stood fast and made a fight of it.

Managing to check his prancing mount at last, Pistol-whipper yelled something unintelligible to his companion, then did the very last thing O'Brien wanted him to do.

He brought up his Colt and returned fire.

O'Brien saw flame lance from the weapon about half a second before he heard the high, vicious crack of the shot itself, and instinctively swerved his charging mount a little to the left.

Then, when no more than thirty yards separated them, he brought the blood-bay to a wild, slithering halt, turned the horse broadside on and fired again.

Bark exploded off a ponderosa pine to Pistol-whipper's right, showering man and horse alike with thick, reddish splinters and, as the would-be robber buried his head in his shoulders, he yelled, '*Gun 'im, George! Gun the sonofabitch*!'

Figuring that *he* must be the sonofabitch in question, O'Brien quickly brought the Lightning around to make sure he got Pistol-Whipper's buddy, this here George, before George got *him*.

But George wasn't even looking his way.

No — the man in the buggy was his target.

That poor devil was still sprawled across the wagon-seat, one hand holding his bloody face, where Pistol-whipper had struck him, the other still clutching the reins of his frantic team. He was scared and unarmed; a scared, unarmed greenhorn who posed no threat at all to his tormentors, and yet —

And yet they were going to shoot him down in cold blood.

It didn't make any sense.

Kicking his mare a little closer to the buggy, George stabbed his .44 at its cowering occupant, but before he could do any more than that, O'Brien snap-aimed and sent a warning shot over the big man's head, figuring to make him think again.

George wasn't a man to have second thoughts, though, and keeping his eyes fixed on the greenhorn, he thumbed back the hammer and —

With no real choice in the matter, O'Brien shot him in the chest.

The bullet hit the big man with sledgehammer force and thwacked him backwards off his wall-eyed horse and, as he fell groundward, the Remington flew from his hand to clatter among the rocks at the edge of the trail.

Knowing that if he wasn't already

dead, he very soon would be, O'Brien turned his attention back to Pistol-whipper, expecting — *hoping* — to see the man turning-tail and lighting a shuck.

Instead, he found himself staring right down the barrel of his opponent's Cavalry Colt.

He thought, *Damn!* which was pretty mild considering that he'd just used up his fifth and final shot on George, and the Lightning in his fist was now empty.

Hard on the heels of that, he thought about the Winchester .45/.60 in the scabbard under his right leg, although he knew he'd never be able to draw, aim, lever and fire the rifle before Pistol-whipper blew him out of this life and into the next.

All of which left him with only one other weapon to which he had immedi-ate access — a weapon he used without further ado.

He bawled, 'Yee-haah!' again, and the blood-bay beneath him powered forward into a flat-out gallop, all thousand pounds-plus of it headed straight for his adversary.

Above the line of his bandanna, Pistol-whipper's eyes went as wide as wagon-wheels. Then, recovering himself, he tightened rein to hold his own shifting mount steady, thumb-cocked the Cavalry Colt and pulled the trigger.

O'Brien swore he felt the hot wind of the .44/.40 sizzle past his left ear, but still he kept going, yelling at the blood-bay to keep eating up the distance between him and the man who was so keen to kill him; and the blood-bay, good horse that it was, did just that; inch by inch, foot by foot, yard by yard, closing the gap, always closing it —

'Yee-haah! Yee-haah!'

Spooked by all the commotion, Pistol-whipper's horse started going crazy again, and almost before he knew it, Pistol-whipper himself had his hands full just trying to stay in the saddle. With a roar of defiance he fired another shot, an even hastier one this time, and missed again, this time by the prover-bial mile. Then —

— the blood-bay ploughed right into the lighter, nervier pony, shoulder slamming against shoulder with a harsh pistol-crack of sound, and the force of the collision knifed through both animals and their riders, and hammered the wind out of all four.

O'Brien's horse bounced off the pony and stumbled sideways on legs like paper, then started shaking its big head and snapping at the air, in no great hurry to do anything like that ever again. But that was fine with O'Brien, because the blood-bay had already done *enough*.

Pistol-whipper's pony had been rammed backwards by the impact, towards a spot where the trail gave way to a steep, pine-timbered slope that was littered with rocks and deadfall wood and, as the ground appeared to give way beneath it, the animal began to panic even more.

Ears flattening against its head, eyes showing more white than anything else, it dug and clawed to regain its balance on the grade, its legs all over the place. It lurched and recovered, stumbled and plunged, then came up hard against a half-rotted log that was all but hidden in the tall grass and went over with a scream that made O'Brien's jaw clamp hard.

Not wanting to be caught under the falling animal, Pistol-whipper kicked out of the stirrups and threw himself sideways with an oath that was muffled by his bandanna. He landed on legs that were too stiff to absorb the full, jarring force of the fall, and when they crumpled beneath him he pitched forward, losing his hat almost immediately, and started falling ass-over-teakettle down the slope; rolling, yelling, bouncing; rolling, yelling, bouncing; occasionally catching himself on an up-thrust rock or pine-trunk, and leaving in his wake a trail of flattened grass and broken, swaying columbines.

He carried on like that for another dozen yards or so, then suddenly stopped yelling and just continued to bounce and roll in silence, his arms and legs loose now, his body more closely resembling a sack of rags than anything human.

Watching him go, O'Brien wondered grimly whether he'd knocked himself out or killed himself in the fall.

★　★　★

He sat the double-rig for a moment longer, catching his breath. To the west, the setting sun continued to stretch the shadows and colour them purple, and around him a heavy silence that was broken only by the mournful keening of the blustery wind began to reclaim the foothills.

At last he swung down, dropped leather to ground-hitch the quivering blood-bay and set about reloading the Lightning. Almost immediately, the tension of the past two minutes caught up with him, as it always did when the shooting stopped. And, just like always, it threatened to leave him feeling more than a mite quivery himself.

Knowing from experience that the sensation would pass — eventually — he moved past the still skittish wagon-team and reached the edge of the trail just as Pistol-whipper's pony shoved back up on to all fours.

As near as he could tell, the animal had suffered no serious or permanent injury, and he was glad to see it. In fact, aside from a few shallow cuts and grazes to which fallen leaves and twigs now stuck, the horse appeared to have fared considerably better than its rider. It had taken a heavy tumble, crashed onto one side and rolled all the way over, then slipped for several yards before finally managing to dig in and halt the downward slide.

Now, as he finished reloading, set the hammer down on the always empty sixth chamber and deftly reholstered the weapon, the pony began to descend the slope in a series of dainty crow-hops, instinct telling it that it should go in search of its no-good master.

Of Pistol-whipper, however, there was no longer any sign, just the odd, distant rustle of disturbed foliage some 2-300 yards below, where the timber grew thicker and cast deeper, near impenetrable shadows. After a time, even that died away to nothing.

'They . . . they were going to *kill* me,' the man in the buggy said suddenly, making a weird little sound that was laugh and sob all in one.

O'Brien turned to face him. The greenhorn was still sprawled across the single sprung seat, the reins still clutched in one gloved hand, the other still cradling his injured cheek. He was younger than O'Brien had expected, somewhere in his middle-twenties; clean-shaven, lightly tanned and pleas-antly handsome, with a long, straight nose and heart-shaped lips that were now drawn tight at the corners.

'Who were they?' asked O'Brien.

The greenhorn half-climbed, half-fell

down off the buggy, still bewildered by the recent violence. 'They — ' But before he could say any more, however, something in his face, in his scared hazel-green eyes, seemed to close down, and after a pause he finished stiffly, 'Robbers, I guess.'

O'Brien raised one eyebrow. 'You *guess*?'

'Well, who else would they be?' the greenhorn countered defensively.

At last he thought to study his saviour a little more closely, and saw a tall, flat-bellied man on the lee-side of forty, with broad shoulders that tapered to a narrow, gun-hung waist, and lumpy, cauliflowered ears that suggested a hard and sometimes brutal life. Moderating his tone, he said, 'Th-thank you for what you did just now, Mr, ah . . . ?'

'O'Brien.'

'Well, I'm beholden to you, Mr O'Brien. I . . . I owe you my *life*.' Tugging off one of his gloves, the greenhorn thrust out an unsteady hand.

'My name's . . . Collins, by the way. Roy Collins.'

They shook, after which O'Brien went over to the dead man and knelt beside the body. As dispassionately as he could, he tugged the bandanna down off George's jowly, stubble-darkened face and studied it for a moment. In death, the big man's near-black eyes had crossed, and the bright scarlet blood he'd coughed up with his dying breath still glistened wetly on his thick lips.

Working quickly, he went through the pockets of the dead man's mackinaw, came up with a tarnished pocket watch, a box of strike-anywheres and the makings, about twelve dollars in paper and coin, and not much of anything else.

'Why do you suppose him and his partner were so set on killing you?' he asked, as he shoved back to his feet.

The greenhorn glanced away from him. 'Perhaps they thought . . . I don't know. That I had a gun. That I was reaching for it.'

O'Brien took off his hat and ran his fingers up through his close-cropped salt-and-pepper hair. That could have been the way of it, of course. And he had no real reason, other than good, old-fashioned gut-instinct, to suspect otherwise. But the greenhorn's hands had been busy right through the whole donny-brook, one holding his gashed cheek, the other holding his reins. At no time had he presented a threat, just a target.

He couldn't help but wonder why that should be.

The dead man's chestnut mare was standing with its head down about twenty yards away. He walked over to the animal and caught up the trailing reins. Soothing the jittery horse with nonsense words, he checked through George's saddle-bags, but once again came up empty.

Reaching a decision, he led the mare back to the buggy. 'Where are you headed, Collins?'

Again the greenhorn started to form

a reply, only to suddenly bite off whatever he'd been about to say.

'Collins?' he prodded.

Almost grudgingly, the greenhorn murmured, 'Elkhorn.'

O'Brien thought he'd heard of the place. It was a middling-sized cattle town about thirty, forty miles to the south and west. 'Then we're headed in the same direction, leastways till we reach Skeeter Creek,' he announced. 'We can ride that far together, if you've a mind. And if your friend here was from around these parts, the law there might be able to tell us who he was.'

'I'd welcome the company,' Collins confessed, throwing an uneasy glance around him. 'Truth to tell, Mr O'Brien, this high country seems to have taken on a rather ... *sinister* air, all of a sudden.'

That settled, O'Brien rolled George into a seen-better-days blanket he took from behind the dead man's cantle, then used his lariat to tie the bundle together. When he was finished, he told the greenhorn to give him a hand boosting the body up across his saddle, where O'Brien then tied it in place, wrist-to-ankle beneath the mare's belly.

While he was occupied thus, Collins wandered across to the waiting blood-bay and began to examine the heavy, slab-like muscles that made up the animal's left shoulder. Curiously, O'Brien watched him work. He had a gentle touch and looked like he knew what he was doing, and the blood-bay — who could be an ornery cuss when he wanted to be — didn't seem to mind his attentions in the least.

'He'll have some nasty bruising for a while,' the greenhorn reported, as he led the horse around to the back of the buggy a few minutes later. 'You'd best go easy on him for a while, till he heals.'

O'Brien had just finished tying the mare's reins to the buggy's boot-rail. Now he took those of the blood-bay and repeated the procedure. 'I will,' he replied. 'I'll ride in the buggy with you, till we find a place to make camp.'

'Right.'

As they climbed into the rig, O'Brien said, 'You talk like a man who knows his way around horses.'

Collins' response was a brief, self-conscious little shrug. 'Some,' he replied, as he kicked off the brake and got them moving again. But more than that he wouldn't say.

Frowning, O'Brien snuck his companion a brief sidelong glance. He got the feeling that there was more to Roy Collins than met the eye — maybe a lot more. But it was equally clear that the greenhorn wasn't about to give away any more about himself than he had to, not even to the man who'd just saved his life.

Which left O'Brien with an obvious question to ponder.

Just what was it that Roy Collins had to hide?

2

They reached Skeeter Creek a little after noon the following day.

The town stretched across the floor of a steepsided valley that was cut through the middle by the none-too-clean stream that gave the place its name. The stream also served as a kind of natural barrier between the town proper, which had stood there for twenty years or more, and the messy jumble of cabins, dugouts, tents and lean-tos which had sprung up following the discovery of precious metal in the region.

Hauling rein while they were still a quarter-mile off, Collins brought his buggy to halt on a gentle rise in the trail and muttered a soft, awestruck, 'My God.'

Once, the valley had been a place of great natural beauty. Belt upon belt of aspen, fir and spruce had covered its hills in fragrant, serried ranks, and the creek itself had chuckled east-to-west as clear as glass.

But not any more.

Four months earlier, the twin discoveries of gold in the creek and silver carbonate in the surrounding hills had put Skeeter Creek on the map in no uncertain terms, and though the gold hadn't really amounted to much — leastways not *yet* — there was talk that the hills held what promised to be the biggest yield of silver carbonate seen in those parts since the glory days of Leadville, a decade earlier.

That prospect alone had drawn newcomers to the valley in their hundreds, and with the arrival of every miner, schemer, dreamer, soiled dove and would-be tycoon, the place had changed beyond all recognition. Now, the slopes were scarred with great, barren patches where the timber had been slashed to make way for crude roadways, mineshafts and equipment, and the once-pristine creek ran slack and murky, its banks peppered with grubby, whiskery men using pans, rockers and sluices to sift its waters in search of colour.

O'Brien didn't believe he'd ever seen anything quite so ugly.

Collins evidently agreed, because he quickly got them moving again, down through the noisy, stinking, overcrowded confusion of the mining camp, across the bridge that spanned the creek and on into the town beyond, with the two tethered saddlemounts trotting along behind them, and George's corpse still hanging belly-down across the mare.

Main Street was a wide, busy thoroughfare set between facing rows of plank-built stores, saloons and restaurants. The sheriff's office — a squat log building with a flat board roof and a small barred window set either side of a sturdy central door — stood about midway along the east side of the street, and was identified as such by a flaking shingle that read:

SHERIFF'S OFFICE
J.B. TUCKER
TAX COLLECTOR
HEALTH, FIRE,
SANITATION INSPECTOR

An overweight but still powerfully built man in his early sixties was seated in an old board-and-rawhide chair to one side of the door. The mottled brass star pinned to his grey flannel shirt identified him as the aforementioned J.B. Tucker, and he'd been watching the constant flow of wagon and horseback traffic from beneath the shade of a round-crowned black hat until Collins pulled the buggy to a stop in front of his office. Then he turned his head their way — and his mild blue eyes narrowed down when he saw who was on the seat.

'O'Brien?' he murmured with a frown. Then, shoving up and lumbering across the boardwalk as fast as his bulk would allow, 'By thunder, it is you 'neath all that chin-hair! Lord A'mighty, man,

I ain't seen you in years — *two*, at th' least!'

O'Brien climbed down to share a strong clasp of hands with him. 'I'll be damned — Joe Tucker! How you been keeping, Joe?'

'Leanin' forward all the way,' the sheriff replied as they shook. 'But what about *you*? Hear tell you found yourself a fat Mexican woman an' settled down someplace around Nacozari!'

'I *wish*,' O'Brien said with a laugh.

'Well, maybe I'm confusin' you with some other no-good, fiddle-footed gun-hand of my acquaintance. That happens when you start notchin' up the years. Still an' all, it's good to see you, Carter.'

O'Brien, who was rarely if ever addressed by his first name, gestured to the star on the other man's chest. 'Still packing tin, I see. Thought you might've retired by now.'

'Man has to do what he does best,' the lawman allowed with a shrug, 'an' do it as long as he's able.' Then his eyes ticked briefly to the chestnut mare and her blanket-wrapped burden, and the smile seemed to drop right off his face. 'Curious-lookin' piece o' freight you're totin' there,' he observed mildly. 'Looks to be a man, lessen I miss my guess. But a man who's deader'n a bee in a blizzard.'

O'Brien nodded, also sobering. 'Thought you might be able to tell us who he was, Joe.'

From his place on the sprung seat, Collins watched them go around to the rear of the wagon, where the lawman pulled back the blanket, grabbed a fistful of George's long black hair and lifted his head to get a better look at his face.

'George Weedon,' he said almost immediately, and made a sour expression with his mouth. 'Your doin'?'

'It was him or Roy Collins, here.'

The sheriff glanced at the greenhorn for the first time and asked, 'What happened?'

Squirming a little at the memory,

Collins briefly recounted the events of the previous afternoon. At the end of it, Tucker let the blanket drop back over the dead man's face and opined, 'Well, whatever George Weedon got at your hands, O'Brien, he had it comin' — in spades.'

'Who was he, Joe?'

'A belly-crawlin', sonofabitch bastard, that's who. Rustler, whiskey peddler, gun-for-hire. You name it, he's tried it, one time or another.'

'Well, he's yours now,' said O'Brien, untying the mare's reins from the boot-rail and handing them to the lawman, 'and you're welcome to him. You'll find about twelve bucks in his pockets. That ought to buy him a pine box, I reckon.'

The sheriff took the proffered reins and wrapped them around his knuckly left hand. 'I'll see to it. That what brought you to Skeeter Creek?'

'That, and the prospect of a job, if I can find one.'

'Well, there's plenty of those to be

had. As you can see, we got us quite a boom hereabouts.' Suddenly he frowned. 'What happened to the other feller, by the way? Collins here said there was two of 'em.'

Remembering Pistol-whipper's fate, O'Brien threw a brief glance at George Weedon and said, 'Things went downhill for *him*, too.'

The sheriff fixed him with a shrewd look. 'That has a habit of happenin' to folks who try mixin' it up with you, I've noticed. But much as I'd like to stand here just a-shootin' the breeze, I think I'd better have one o' my boys take the deceased here down to Dan Stephensen's funeral parlour. 'Case you hadn't noticed, the sonofabitch's startin' to reek somethin' fierce.'

As they shook hands again, Tucker said softly, 'You come on back when you've got yourself settled, Carter, an' we'll yarn awhile.' Then he turned away and bellowed, '*Chuck! Get on out here, I got a chore for you!*'

While he issued orders to the deputy

who came running, O'Brien untied his own reins and led the blood-bay around to the side of the buggy.

'Is that *it*?' Collins asked, when he was close enough.

O'Brien frowned. 'What did you expect?'

'Well . . . I'm not sure, really. I thought . . . I mean — a man's life . . . I just naturally assumed there'd be a coroner's inquest or something.'

'Well, that's the thing about living in a boomtown,' O'Brien replied. 'Nine times out of ten, you're more likely to get the 'or something' part.'

Collins shook his head as he considered that, the ways of the West still a mystery to him. Then he said, 'I suppose this is where we, ah, part the ways, then?'

O'Brien offered his right hand. 'I suppose it *is*.'

'Well, thank you again for, well . . . '

'Forget it.'

'That's hardly likely. You had to kill a man — two men — because of me. And that can't have been an easy thing, I know.'

'It wasn't,' O'Brien allowed. 'But let's just say that I killed two bad men to save one *good* one, shall we?'

At that, Collins glanced away from him momentarily, his lips drawing tight and his jaw muscles bunching briefly. When he looked back again, he said impulsively, 'Mr O'Brien — '

'Uh-huh?'

For a long couple of seconds, the greenhorn looked him in the face, his mouth working silently, like that of a fish on a riverbank. He wanted to say . . . *something*. But whatever it was, it just wouldn't come. Instead he finally managed, 'So long. And good luck to you.'

Then, with another brief nod, he slapped the reins against his horses' necks, and the buggy jerked away into traffic.

*　*　*

O'Brien booked himself into a hotel down at the northern end of Main and made arrangements for the care of his horse at the livery next door. A shave came next, at the first, least-busy tonsorial parlour he came to, followed by an all-over bath. After that he started feeling almost human again, but just to complete the transformation, he went in search of a café and ordered his first home-cooked meal in more than a week. *En route*, he also picked up a copy of the Skeeter Creek *Record*.

While he waited for his meal to come — and it took a while, because the place was jammed solid — he scanned the flimsy newspaper to see if he could get a handle on who was hiring hereabouts. The paper suggested a couple of possibilities he thought he might check out, but the emphasis was more on national news than anything else. There was an article on the Mormon practice of polygamy and Washington's continuing efforts to stamp it out, another on the latest attempt by the Committee for Indian Affairs to civilize the red man, and a report on the previous year's outbreak of hoof-and-mouth to the south-west, which had all but destroyed the state's cattle industry. This last snippet also explained why the cafe's owner had tacked a rough-and-ready sign to the door that read NO MEAT CEPT CHICKEN.

After a tolerable meal of the aforementioned fowl and boiled potatoes, he took a stroll around town, just to get a feel for the place and see for himself what opportunities it might offer. A recently constructed stamp-mill sat on the far south-eastern slope, from which issued a constant, hammering *thud*, and a pall of dirty, sulphurous smelter-smoke.

It was coming on dusk when he started back to his hotel, and Skeeter Creek's pole-toting lamp-lighter was slowly working his way along Main, opening the gas-valve in each low streetlamp in turn so that he could then light the jet. O'Brien had spotted the modest gas works itself, with its complicated-looking generating equipment, on his earlier tour of town.

He let himself into his room — a small, sparsely-furnished affair with gaudy wallpaper depicting a series of grapevines upon which perched various birds of plumage — took off his hat and jacket, unbuckled his gunbelt and set them all on a chair beside the bed. Then he lit the coal-oil lamp and opened the window, and was taking one final look at the busy street below when there came a discreet rapping at the door. With a frown, for he was still largely unknown around town and wasn't expecting visitors, he crossed the room to answer it.

'Ah, Mr O'Brien. I . . . I hope I'm not, ah, disturbing you . . . '

It was Roy Collins.

Recovering from his surprise — because the greenhorn was the last person he'd been expecting to see again — O'Brien shook his head. 'You're not. But I figured you'd be halfway to Elkhorn by now. Change your mind?'

Another of those fleeting, self-conscious little smiles ghosted across the other man's heart-shaped mouth as he stood just beyond the threshold, turning his hat nervously by its narrow brim. 'Yes, I . . . decided to stop over for a, uh, day or so.' His hazelgreen eyes shuttled briefly to a spot beyond O'Brien's shoulder, and he said, 'I wondered if I might, ah, have a word?'

O'Brien took a backward step. 'Come on in.'

'You're a difficult man to find,' Collins remarked as he halted in the centre of the room. 'It's taken me all afternoon to track you down. I didn't think there could be so many hotels and boarding-houses in one town.'

'But you managed it in the end,' replied O'Brien. 'Mind if I ask why?'

The greenhorn didn't answer immediately. He just stood there, clutching his hat so tightly now that his knuckles started to show white. His face, too, looked pale against the rusty brown of his suit, pale even against the whiteness of his boiled shirt, at the neck of which he wore a black string tie.

Then, almost visibly screwing up his courage, he said, 'Well, to begin with, I should like to make a . . . a small confession. You have shown me nothing but kindness, Mr O'Brien, and I in turn . . . well, let's just say that I haven't been entirely . . . *open* with you.'

'Oh?'

'Yes. You see, my name . . . it's not Roy Collins. It's Rae Caulder.'

It meant nothing to O'Brien, who asked only, 'Why'd you lie about it?'

'To be honest with you — and this is going to sound terrible, given that you saved my life yesterday, and I shall be eternally in your debt for so doing — I wasn't sure just how far I could, ah, *trust* you.'

O'Brien smiled sourly. 'Well, that's honest enough. What changed your mind?'

'Sheriff Tucker. I . . . made some enquiries, you see, shortly after we said our, ah, goodbyes this afternoon. And he spoke very highly of you. Very highly indeed. He called you a man with bark on him, and absolutely no quit. Those were his exact words. He said that you were a fighting man by trade, a sort of gun-for-hire, and that when you take a job, you see it through, no matter what.'

'So you came here tonight . . . ?' prodded O'Brien.

'To offer you a job,' said Caulder, adding, 'I should like you to, uh, protect me. Until I reach Elkhorn.'

O'Brien felt himself frowning again. 'If you're still fretting about what happened yesterday, forget it. You're not likely to run into the likes of George Weedon again 'twixt here and there, if that's what's on your mind.'

'Nevertheless, it *could* happen. Lightning can strike twice, you know.'

'It's been known, I guess,' O'Brien allowed. 'But you sound to me like a man who *expects* it to strike again — and that makes me wonder just why that should be. If you're in some kind of trouble — '

'I'm not,' the greenhorn replied quickly.

'And yet you lie about your real name, you come close to getting yourself killed by two men you *guess* were robbers, and you half-expect to run into another hardcase or two before you get to where you're going,' O'Brien reminded him. 'What *is* your business in Elkhorn, anyway?'

'That, I'm afraid is, uh, confidential.'

'But whatever it is, someone's determined to stop you getting there. Is that it?'

His guess was so close to the truth that the greenhorn suddenly sagged. 'I didn't think so,' he said in a miserable half-whisper. 'But after yesterday, I'm not so sure.'

'So that business with George and his buddy — they weren't really out to rob you, were they?'

'I *thought* they were, at first. I mean, why else would they wear masks and brandish guns? But when they started talking, I realized that what they really wanted was for me to . . . to turn back, or else.'

'What did they say, exactly?'

'I'm sorry, Mr O'Brien, but I can't tell you that. I gave my word that I would discuss the, ah, task for which I have been employed, with no one.'

'That leaves us in a fix, then, doesn't it?' O'Brien said with a sigh. 'Because I never hire out until I know *something*, at least, about why I'm risking my neck — and you're not in any position to tell me.'

'All I'm asking is that you . . . you 'ride shotgun' on me until I reach Elkhorn,' Caulder returned plaintively.

But O'Brien saw it a different way. 'What you're asking me to do is sign up to a gun job without knowing the first thing about who or what I might have to go up against,' he countered. 'And that's something I'm not prepared to do.'

'If it's a question of money — '

'It's not.'

'But if it *was*,' the greenhorn persisted, 'I'm sure the people who've hired me would be more than happy to make it worth your while.'

O'Brien shook his head. 'Just let it ride, Caulder,' he replied, his voice taking on a harder edge. 'I'm not interested, and there's an end to it.'

A heavy silence that was broken only by the distant thumping of the stamp-mill descended over the room. Five or ten seconds passed more like five or ten minutes, until Caulder said, 'Then all I can do is, ah, thank you for your time. Good . . . goodnight, Mr O'Brien. I'm sorry to have, uh, troubled you.'

He let himself out and closed the door softly behind him.

After he'd gone, O'Brien went back to the window and looked down into the street below. It was full dark now, but beneath the sickly amber glow of the streetlamps, Main Street was still bustling. Half a minute passed, and then Caulder came out of the hotel and paused on the boardwalk. O'Brien watched him put his hat on, then cross the street, dodging the steady stream of wagon and horseback traffic to reach the far side. Once there, he headed south at a slow, preoccupied walk, head bowed, shoulders slumped, a picture of despair.

O'Brien wondered briefly if he'd been too hard on the man. Maybe. But what was he *supposed* to do? The more he'd heard about Caulder's proposition — which wasn't a whole damn' lot, it had to be said — the less he'd wanted anything to do with it.

He was just about to turn away from the window when his attention was taken by a man who suddenly detached himself from the shadows of an alley-mouth Caulder had just passed. Even as he watched, the man started limping along in the greenhorn's wake.

Eyes narrowing, O'Brien leaned a little closer to the glass.

The man was of average height, with longish, light-coloured hair that spilled down from beneath a high-crowned hat to curl over the collar of his black peacoat.

O'Brien heard himself mutter, 'I'll be damned . . . '

It was Pistol-whipper.

So the sonofabitch had survived his tumble yesterday, after all. Survived it, caught up the horse that had gone down after him and then trailed Collins — that was, *Caulder* — all the way to Skeeter Creek.

And there could only be one reason for that.

He was planning to finish what he and George Weedon had started the previous afternoon.

Jaw setting hard, O'Brien pushed away from the window, snatched up his gunbelt and left the room at a sprint. A few moments later, still buckling the gunbelt back around his waist, he burst out onto Main and into a night which had cooled considerably.

Throwing caution aside, he leapt straight down into the street itself, narrowly avoiding a knock from a passing Murphy wagon and causing a startled rider to rein in fast and tell him to watch the hell where he was going.

Then he reached the far boardwalk,

and had to slow to a steadier stride so that he wouldn't collide with any shuffling miners and dawdling towns-folk.

Moving on as fast as he could, settling the hang of the .38 just right against his hip, he scanned the crowd ahead for sign of his quarry. A moment later he spotted Pistol-whipper about thirty yards ahead, with Caulder ten yards further on. Pistol-whipper was moving faster now: leastways, as fast as his gimpy leg would allow. *Closing in for the kill*, he thought, wondering if the man had injured his leg in yesterday's fall, or come by his limp some other way.

Next minute, Pistol-whipper came up behind Caulder, and Caulder still didn't have the first clue that he was there. He reached out and clamped his gloved right hand on the greenhorn's shoulder, and O'Brien saw Caulder break stride, turn his head —

The greenhorn's hazel-green eyes widened in shock.

Quickly, before he could do or say anything about it, Pistol-whipper drew level with him. From a distance, they looked like old friends, one with his arm around the other. Then Pistol-whipper started moving again, drawing Caulder along with him, until they reached an alleyway between two tall, plank-built stores ten yards further on. There, Pistol-whipper suddenly turned left, dragging the reluctant greenhorn into the narrow thoroughfare with him.

Knowing there was no time to lose now, that this business — however it had come about — was rapidly reaching its inevitable conclusion, O'Brien broke into a trot, reaching down as he went, sliding the Colt from leather, drawing back the hammer —

An eternity later he reached the alley, turned into it. It was black with shadow. Willing his eyes to adjust to the darkness, he quickly side-stepped to the right, so that he would blend with the wall there and not be outlined against the lighter street, behind him.

A few crates had been stacked along the left-side wall, about forty feet ahead, but that was all he could really make out. There was no sign of Pistol-whipper, no sign of Caulder. Then —

'. . . *please* . . . '

It was Caulder's voice, soft, high, desperate, coming from a spot just beyond the crates.

Instantly he picked up the pace, all the while trying to make as little noise as possible. He ghosted forward with his back to the wall and his eyes to the front until, at last, he saw them twenty feet away.

Pistol-whipper had shoved Caulder up against the left-side wall and was pinning him there with his left hand, which was splayed against the green-horn's narrow chest. In his right he held a slim, long-bladed knife, the point of which he was pressing up into the soft flesh just under Caulder's jaw.

'. . . could'a done this the easy way, an' no harm done,' O'Brien heard him hiss through clenched teeth, 'but oh no, you had to make things difficult, di'n't you? Well, that's jus' dandy. You can die just as easy down here as in them hills, Doctor-man — '

Having heard enough, O'Brien came away from the wall and snapped, 'Don't even *think* about it!'

Pistol-whipper twitched at the sudden bark of sound, turned fast at the waist, and even though the light was poor, O'Brien got a good-enough first look at him.

He wasn't a pretty sight. The face he'd hidden behind his bandanna the day before was long and thin, just sunken eyes and prominent cheekbones and a sharp hatchet-blade of a nose. The features were grazed and bruised now, of course, the result of yesterday's crazy descent through the rocks and timber. The lid of his left eye had swollen up, and the skin surrounding it was an angry mixture of red and purple. His lips were puffed up, too, emphasizing the sneer into which they had formed.

But it was the eyes that held O'Brien's attention most of all. The right one, at least, saucered: first in surprise, then in fear — then in recognition.

He spat, '*You!*'

And then he threw the knife.

He threw it fast, in a low underarm sweep, not for one moment expecting it to hit O'Brien, but sure as hell hoping that it would distract him while he grabbed for the .44 at his hip.

O'Brien, expecting such a move, quickly dodged to one side and yelled, '*Caulder — get down!*'

A gunblast shattered the stillness then, as Pistol-whipper thumbed off his first shot even before his Cavalry Colt had properly cleared leather, and magnified by the confines of the dogtrot, it sounded more like the roar of a cannon. Hard on the heels of that he fired again, but this shot, like its predecessor, went wide.

Again O'Brien yelled, '*Caulder!*'

And this time, whatever spell had

been holding the greenhorn right there in the line of fire finally broke. He dropped low, and at last O'Brien had the chance he'd been waiting for — to shoot back without hitting the very man he was hoping to save.

He fanned the Lightning twice, once above Pistol-whipper's last muzzle-flash, once below it, the two reports coming so close together that they sounded more like one.

Lead cored Caulder's would-be killer through the upper chest and lower stomach, bent him in two and slammed him backwards, into the wall. He hit the weathered planks hard, made a weird kind of gulping sound, then pitched face-first on to the ground, where he squirmed a bit, then finally lay still.

Letting his pent-up breath go in a hiss, O'Brien came forward at a slow walk, gun still in hand. Caulder, down on his knees a yard or so from the body, watched his approach through terrified eyes.

'I . . . ' he began, 'I . . . '

O'Brien said, 'It's all right, Caulder. It's over.'

He knelt beside the body, turned it over, felt for a pulse, found nothing. But the face . . . Now that he was able to take a longer, closer look at it, Pistol-whipper seemed somehow *familiar* to him, as if he'd seen him before, someplace: certainly before yesterday.

The rest of the world came flooding back in, then — the skin-tightening chill of the evening air; the arsenic-laden stink of smelter-smoke it carried with it; a low, excited buzz of conversation nearby.

Glancing over one shoulder, he saw that the alley-mouth was beginning to fill with curious towners who'd been drawn by the gunfire. Ignoring them, he stood up, ejected the spent, still-warm shell casings from the .38 and began to feed in fresh rounds.

He had the damnedest feeling that, if he didn't part ways with Caulder real soon, he was going to need every ounce of lead he could lay his hands on.

3

Joe Tucker and two of his deputies turned up about three minutes later. One of them — earlier that afternoon, O'Brien had heard Tucker call him Chuck — was carrying a storm lantern, held high. Together, the three of them shoved through the crowd and came to a halt above the corpse. Tucker took one look at the body, one look at Caulder, one look at O'Brien, and then said, 'Well?'

Since Caulder was in no fit state to answer the question, O'Brien did all the talking.

'So this is the second man,' Tucker summarized when he'd finished. 'The one you thought you'd killed yesterday, when him an' George Weedon tried to rob Collins, here?'

O'Brien nodded.

'He must've had a powerful hate for

you, Collins,' the sheriff remarked. 'Comin' all this way, knocked about as he was, just to settle the score.'

'I guess he blamed Collins for his misfortunes,' said O'Brien, when Caulder made no move to reply.

'Maybe,' replied Tucker, his tone sceptical. 'But why go after Collins, when it was *you* that shoved him down that hill?'

'I was probably next on his list.'

'Could be,' the sheriff allowed, still dubious. 'Anyway, it sure was lucky for Collins here that you happened to spot him.'

Upon his arrival, Tucker had quickly taken command of the situation. While one of his deputies dispersed the crowd and then went in search of the knife O'Brien had told him should be around there someplace, the other went to fetch the mortician, leaving Tucker himself to hold the lantern shoulder-high.

Now, with shadows puddled around their feet and filling their eye-sockets, the lawman nudged Pistol-whipper with the tip of one boot and said confidentially, 'You know who this *hombre* is, don't you?'

'I wasn't sure at first,' O'Brien admitted, 'but it's Al Grandee, isn't it?'

'Yup. Tom Grandee's kid brother, an' the apple of his eye.' Tucker made a tutting sound deep in his throat. 'There'll be ructions over this when Tom gets to hear about it. You know Tom Grandee. Ain't never been right in th'head since he lost his arm down on the Rosebud. An' even before that he was so damn' ornery he'd shoot a man jus' for the pleasure of seein' him fall.'

'Is he in the territory?' asked O'Brien.

'Could be. If Al was here, I don't s'pose Tom'd be too far away.'

Just then Chuck came stomping back over, a knife balanced in the palm of his outstretched hand. 'Found it, Joe.'

The sheriff took it with a nod, then threw another glance at Caulder. 'You all right, there, Collins? You're still lookin' a mite green 'bout the gills.'

Caulder swallowed. 'I . . . I'll be all right. It was just a . . . a shock, that's all.'

'Well, from what I've heard, what Chuck here jus' found, an' what I already know of the mean nature of the deceased, I'm satisfied that O'Brien acted in defence of your life an' his own. But since this all took place in my bailiwick, as against your earlier run-in with George Weedon, I'll need you to put it all in writin'. You too, Carter. Best you both stop by my office first thing in the mornin', get this business squared away.'

O'Brien nodded tiredly. 'We'll be there, Joe.'

A few minutes later the mortician and his assistant arrived, carrying a wide board between them. As they watched, Al Grandee, the sonofabitch formerly known as Pistol-whipper, was rolled onto the makeshift gurney, covered with a dark blanket and carried away. Joe Tucker and his deputies trailed after them, leaving O'Brien,

Caulder and the alley-way itself in near-darkness.

'I thought my last moment had come,' Caulder said in a shock-deadened voice. 'If you hadn't — '

'But I *did*,' O'Brien cut in, more harshly than he meant to. The thumping of the stamp-mill was making him feel edgy and restless, or maybe it was just reaction to the recent violence. Pulling down a deep breath, he continued wearily, 'Go on back to wherever it is you're staying, lock yourself in and get some sleep. I'll see you down at Joe's office in the morning.'

Caulder nodded. 'All . . . all right.'

'And once we've seen to all the paperwork,' O'Brien added softly, 'I'm taking you to Elkhorn.'

The greenhorn froze in the act of straightening his tie and stared at him, mouth agape. 'You . . . you've changed your mind about my proposal, then?' he breathed, hardly daring to believe it. 'You'll take the job after all?'

'I mean I've just killed two men on your account,' O'Brien told him harshly. '*That's* why I've decided to haul your sorry hide to Elkhorn, Caulder, because I want to know *why*.'

★ ★ ★

He was as good as his word, too, and after making and signing their statements early the following morning, he and Caulder quit town, headed south and west.

As he settled himself more comfortably into his old Texas double-rig, O'Brien decided that he wasn't entirely sorry to be leaving Skeeter Creek so soon. He'd come to town with the intention of selling his gun to the highest bidder, and had figured his chances of finding well-paid gun-work to be good. In towns like Skeeter Creek, it always *was*, because gold and silver strikes didn't only make men rich, they also made them targets for *other* men: hard and ruthless men who would stop at pretty much nothing to take those riches away from them.

For the right price, O'Brien would do his damnedest to make sure that didn't happen. And, if past experience was any indicator, his damnedest was usually good *enough*.

But somewhere along the line he'd forgotten that he was, first and foremost, a man of the great open spaces. And though he could be sociable enough when the mood was upon him, he'd known from the outset that he'd go crazy if he had to spend any length of time in Skeeter Creek.

So he was almost glad to be shaking the boom-town's dust from his heels that morning — and more than a mite curious about just what he'd find waiting for him up ahead.

Not that Caulder was giving away much on that score. Once he'd settled down a touch and stopped seeing killers behind every rock, he was companionable enough, but not once would he be drawn upon the nature of his business in Elkhorn. When O'Brien asked him why Al Grandee had called him *doctor-man* the previous night, he just raised his eyebrows innocently and said, 'Did he?' Neither did he have any idea who'd hired Grandee and George Weedon to stop him from reaching his destination — or so he claimed.

'I figure we'll raise Elkhorn by suppertime,' O'Brien announced, when they spelled the horses at noon. 'Maybe a little before.'

Caulder considered that for a moment, then murmured, 'We're not actually, ah, *headed* for Elkhorn, Mr O'Brien.'

That brought him a long, searching look. 'Are we about to get another one of your 'small confessions'?' asked O'Brien.

Ignoring the sarcasm, Caulder replied, 'We're bound for a ranch some dozen or so miles south of town. Jane Farrow's Long Branch.'

The woman's name made O'Brien narrow his eyes warily. 'Lady rancher?' he asked suspiciously.

'As I understand it, Mrs Farrow took over the business when her husband died. Now she runs it with her sister.'

O'Brien blew air through his lips. *Two* lady ranchers, then. He didn't much like the sound of that, though he was damned if he could really say why. 'Anything else you think I should know while we're about it?' he enquired.

'I don't think so.'

'Well, let's make tracks, then.'

The miles fell behind them and O'Brien continued to keep a watchful eye on their surroundings. Now that they were out of the high country, the land unfurled in a series of vast, rolling prairies salted with the pinks and scarlets of fleabane and rosecrown, and the blustery wind which had torn through the high passes was replaced by an altogether gentler breeze, so that it finally started feeling more like spring and less like winter.

But as the long afternoon stretched on, his thoughts returned to a subject around which they had been revolving, off and on, all day — Al Grandee.

Joe Tucker had said there would be ructions when Al's brother, Tom, heard the news of Al's death. O'Brien himself reckoned that was putting it mildly.

He knew Tom Grandee vaguely. Their paths had crossed a time or two when they'd both been scouting for the army out of Fort Abraham Lincoln. Tom had always been a snake-mean kind of man, the sort who never forgot and never, ever forgave. And now that O'Brien thought about it, he remembered that Al had shared Tom's same grudge-toting nature. A hair-trigger, unpredictable sonofabitch, Al had lacked any kind of warmth, save where his brother was concerned.

And the feeling was mutual. Al was probably the only thing in the world that Tom cared a damn for. So there would be ructions indeed when Tom heard about Al's death. And there'd be no avoiding the clash that was bound to follow when he finally came gunning for O'Brien as, sooner or later, he was cast-iron certain to do.

By late afternoon they began to follow an unmarked trail due south across a series of gentle hills covered with grass of practically every type, from bluestem to grama. It was magnificent country, well-watered and with timber a'plenty, but the range wasn't just under-stocked, it was absolutely devoid of life.

Casting a critical eye from horizon to horizon, O'Brien realized that the article he'd read in the Skeeter Creek *Record* hadn't exaggerated the situation one bit. The previous autumn's outbreak of hoof-and-mouth really had devastated the cattle industry hereabouts.

Directly ahead, and still a couple of miles off, sat a squat ranch house built from two-inch boards, flanked by two corrals, a bunkhouse, cookshack and barn. Although it was dwarfed by the jumble of grass-and-granite hills that piled against the blue April sky behind it, the house looked to be a fair size, and though it had an empty, uninhabited look — at least from this distance — pale-grey smoke drifted skyward from the metal stove-pipe set into its pitched, split-shingle roof, to signify occupancy.

'Long Branch?' Caulder asked expectantly.

O'Brien nodded. 'I reckon.'

They entered the yard about twenty minutes later, scattering the chickens that had been strutting around, searching for the last of that day's dried corn. To one side of the house, someone had worked hard to cultivate a vegetable garden with a flower border. Behind it, a tall windmill turned slowly in the gentle breeze. And though no one had come out to watch their approach, O'Brien had little doubt that unseen eyes had followed them every step of the way in.

Sure enough, as soon as he drew rein before the house, and Caulder stepped on the brake to bring his buggy to a halt beside him, the door swung open and two women stepped out onto the warped veranda, each holding a rifle across her chest.

A boy of about ten, with red hair and freckles, followed them as far as the door, where he watched the newcomers through serious green eyes. His resemblance to the first of the women was unmistakable. Before anyone could speak, however, a soft, dry creak broke the heavy silence, and from the corner of his vision, O'Brien saw the barn door to his right ease open a tad, and the blued barrel of yet another saddle-gun slide forward into the amber slant of late afternoon sunshine.

Everyone studied everyone else for a long moment. Then the first of the women said, 'Dr Caulder?'

O'Brien glanced at his companion. There it was again — *doctor*.

The greenhorn nodded. 'And you would be Mrs Farrow?'

'I'm Jane Farrow, yes, and this is my sister, Lyn Merrick.'

They were tall, these women, though Jane Farrow was taller than her sister by a full three inches. A solid-looking woman with broad shoulders, what looked to be a firm, muscular body, a trim waist and a set of hips that flared attractively beneath the folds of her split riding skirt, she was somewhere in her late thirties, with high, well-defined cheekbones beneath gentle but sad green eyes, and lips that were set in a very slight pout, like those of a woman constantly facing tough decisions and hoping always to make the right one.

Her sister, Lyn Merrick, was younger than her by a decade. And unlike Jane, whose lustrous copper-coloured hair was gathered into a compact bun at the back of her head, Lyn wore her auburn locks loose, so that they fell in a cascade around her oval face, which was sunned to the colour of a new penny.

She and her sister were both striking examples of womanhood, but there were neither silks nor satins here to accentuate their femininity. Long Branch was — *had* been, before the hoof-and-mouth — a working ranch, and these women were dressed for just *that*, especially Lyn, whose slim, toned body was hidden beneath a grey placket shirt tucked into Kentucky jeans, the jeans held up by wide red galluses.

O'Brien realized then that Lyn had been treating him to a similar scrutiny. 'An' you?' she demanded.

'This is Mr O'Brien,' said Caulder, before O'Brien could speak. 'I had some, uh, trouble on the way here. In fact, I wouldn't be here at all, had it not been for Mr O'Brien.'

Stiffening a little, Jane Farrow asked urgently, 'What happened? Did you go through town? I thought we told you — '

'I came straight here, as instructed,' said Caulder. 'But two men stopped me on the trail the day before yesterday. They wore masks, and I thought they intended to rob me. Instead, they warned me against coming here.'

'That how you came by that cut on your cheek?' asked Lyn.

'Yes. And I'd have been injured a lot

worse than that if Mr O'Brien here hadn't taken a hand. Those men would have killed me to stop me from coming here.'

'What happened to them?' It was Lyn again.

'Mr *O'Brien* happened to them,' said Caulder, grimly. 'Now, you people hired me to do a job, but there's obviously more to this business than you've told me, and I want to know what it is before I — '

'Hush, you!' snapped Lyn. 'You were sworn to secrecy, Caulder. No call to go shootin' your mouth off in front of strangers.'

'*Strangers!*' Caulder repeated, aghast. 'I don't think you quite understand, Miss Merrick. Mr O'Brien isn't a *stranger*. He's the man who saved my *life*. And I promised him that he would be well paid for getting me here in one piece.'

'Then I say you took a little too much on yourself,' countered Lyn, anger clouding her otherwise clear hazel eyes. 'Who said you could do that? Who said you could go around spending our money for us? Not that we've got much of that, and certainly not enough to pay fightin' wages.' Her eyes found O'Brien's face again, and she made no attempt to hide the hostility in them. 'I'm sorry, Mr O'Brien,' she said, not sounding sorry at all, 'but it looks as if you've come all this way for nothin'. 'Course, Caulder here can always pay you out of his own pocket, if he likes.'

Caulder treated her to a scornful stare. 'This man saved my — '

'I'll tell you what *this man* is,' snapped Lyn, taking a pace forward. 'He's a stranger, that's what he is. And for all we know, he could just as well be workin' for Lew Glass. You think we're going to welcome him with open arms, tell him all our secrets an' then let him go reportin' everythin' back to that mangy — '

'That's ridiculous!' snapped Caulder. 'This man had to kill two men on my account. On *your* account.'

'An' what does that prove?' demanded

Lyn, raising her eyebrows. 'That he's a killer, that's all.'

A sudden, heavy silence settled back over the yard, until O'Brien, damned if he'd let himself be judged by someone who didn't even know him, gathered up his reins. 'Forget it, Caulder,' he said in a voice like ice. 'All I wanted here were some answers, but I can see now that I'm not apt to get 'em. That being the case, I'll just push along. If one of you, ah, *ladies*, could point me in the direction of town . . . ?'

Jane Farrow, looking embarrassed by her sister's outburst, took a step down into the yard and came to stand by the blood-bay's cheekstrap. Raising one work-toughened hand to shield her eyes from the sunshine, she said, 'Ride north by east for six miles, you'll come to the railroad tracks. Follow them north from there and you'll come to Elkhorn.'

'Obliged.'

'Mr O'Brien?' she said.

'Yes'm?'

'Thank you for what you did. We're

beholden. But these are trying times, and we can't afford to be too careful. I hope you understand.'

'Mrs Farrow,' he replied bluntly, 'I haven't understood a single damn' thing that's happened to me since I ran into *Doctor* Caulder here. But something about you people tells me I'm better off that way.'

Jane Farrow gave him a sad nod. 'I think you *are*,' she said.

Touching his fingers to his hat-brim, O'Brien backed his horse away and turned him around. He saw that a whiskery old man had appeared in the barn doorway, an ill-used Burnside carbine now held loose across his narrow chest. He was sixty if he was a day, and his disreputable old cardigan sweater and striped pants were darkened here and there by what appeared to be grease stains.

For a moment their eyes locked. The old man's were blue and watery, and showed only a fierce desire to protect the women and their property.

O'Brien touched his heels to the blood-bay's flanks and rode out of the yard at a canter.

★   ★   ★

In the fading light of sunset, Elkhorn had a quiet, subdued air that did little to lift his spirits.

He approached the town from the south, crossed the railroad tracks Jane Farrow had mentioned, then skirted a long line of empty, weed-choked shipping pens — reminders of a more prosperous time — until he finally reached the outskirts.

Main Street, he saw, was two facing rows of stores, saloons, hotels and office buildings separated by a wide dirt road, the road bisected every so often by a narrower thoroughfare that gave access to the town's residential district. There was little traffic to speak of — a couple of wagons, some riders, a few towners going about their business, but nothing that came anywhere near the bustle and vitality he'd left behind in Skeeter Creek. And though several stores were still trading, more than a few appeared to have closed for good, their doors now padlocked or crudely boarded up, their windows dark and dusty.

He swung down at the first livery he came to, paid for the care of his horse, then stowed his gear at the back of the barn, promising the stableman that he'd come back for it as soon as he found himself a room for the night.

As he stepped back out onto the street, he tried to decide which of his needs was greater just then — hunger, or thirst. Although they were both pretty pressing, he settled on thirst and headed for a saloon called The Horn A'Plenty, which occupied the corner of the next block over.

A few moments later he pushed into a large, smoke-filled room with a high plank ceiling and a sawdusted floor. To his left, a number of out-of-work cowboys with too much time on their hands were drowning their sorrows at a mahogany-and-brass-rail bar. The rest of the room was given over to a scattering of baize-topped tables and ladderback chairs, at which a few towners nursed drinks or played cards for matches.

All heads turned as the batwings flapped shut behind him, and the muted babble of conversation came to an abrupt halt. In the guttering light of the wagon-wheel chandelier, a line of hard-eyed, distrustful expressions turned his way, and he offered a cautious nod to set them at ease. It seemed to work, because the conversation picked up again as he made his way down to the far, unoccupied end of the bar, and the towners went back to nursing their beers and dealing cards.

The resident mixologist ambled down to serve him. 'What'll it be?' he asked.

'Whiskey. Forty Rod, if you've got it.'

'We got it.'

He dispensed the liquid cheer, scooped up O'Brien's money and then sashayed back to the other end of the bar.

Alone with his thoughts, O'Brien stared moodily into his glass. Much as he hated to admit it, he was still smarting from Lyn Merrick's assessment of him. *He's a killer, that's all*, she'd said. And in a way, she wasn't far from the truth. But he'd never taken another man's life lightly. He killed when he didn't have any other choice, or because he was forced into it, or simply to stop the other feller from killing *him*. Be it right or wrong, that was the nature of the violent business into which he had somehow drifted.

In any case, who was Lyn Merrick to pass judgement on him? She and her sister, up to their eyelashes in secrets and subterfuge? They didn't know him any better than he knew *them*, and they certainly weren't to know just how heavily each of those killings still weighed upon him.

He shook his head in a vain attempt to banish the women from his mind, finished his drink, thought about having another and decided against it. As much as anything else, his belly was reminding him that there was still the small matter of hunger to deal with, so he shoved away from the bar with the intention of hunting up a restaurant. Once he'd eaten his fill, he would find a hotel, book a room, have an early night and push on again at sun-up.

He was halfway to the batwings when three newcomers shoved into the saloon, the high, spur-hung heels of two of them drumming hard against the sawdusted boards as they made their entrance. At the centre of the group was a short, nervous-looking man of about fifty, who was dressed in a green corduroy jacket and grey pants. He was the complete opposite of his two companions, who were both tall, weapon-heavy rangemen.

Since it had worked so well for him the first time, O'Brien offered them a sociable nod and then made to step around them, but even as he did so, one of the rangemen, whose long frame was wrapped in a canvas All-Around duster, suddenly hauled up sharp.

As his associates did likewise, both of them throwing him a curious frown, the man said, 'It's O'Brien, ain't it?' He had a low, unpleasant quality to his voice, like dirt being shovelled on to a coffin-lid.

O'Brien gave him a second, longer look and, as he did so, something cold and disagreeable uncurled inside him. He thought, *Aw, shoot*, or something very much like it, because he knew he should have recognized the man sooner.

It was, in fact, the very last man he wanted to see, then or ever.

It was Pistol-whipper's brother, Tom Grandee.

★ ★ ★

'Hello, Tom,' he said carefully.

Tom Grandee was a tall, gaunt man in his early forties, with a pale, angular face that was now thrown into shade by the brim of his ancient campaign hat. At first glance he didn't look to be much more than skin and bone, but O'Brien knew better. Once, at Fort Abraham Lincoln, he'd seen Tom strip to the waist and wash himself down at a horse trough, and he still remembered the way the muscles had coiled and clung to Tom's narrow frame like so many stout, knotted ropes. Tom Grandee was as tough as nails and as hard as teak, and only a fool would ever think otherwise.

Without warning, Tom's mouth suddenly twisted into a sneer, and it was a moment before O'Brien realized that this was the man's idea of a smile. For just a second Tom's broken, yellow teeth saw the light: then the smile was gone, and the mouth was a straight, lipless slash again.

'Well, well,' he said. 'Fancy runnin' into you.'

O'Brien looked into his cold green eyes — eyes that would have looked more at home in the head of a belligerent cat — and felt his belly muscles tighten still further. 'Yeah,' he replied. 'Fancy.'

Tom wore a blue pullover shirt buttoned to the neck, and brown whipcord britches tucked into well-worn boots. The duster hung from his sloping shoulders like a shroud, unbuttoned so as to give him easy access to the .44-calibre Army Colt he wore buttforward on his right hip, but cinched in tight at the back for a snugger fit. The duster's right sleeve was as near as dammit empty, and he wore it pinned up over the stump where his arm had once been.

He'd lost the arm several years earlier whilst scouting for George Crook up in the Dakota Territory. Crook had been searching for hostile Sioux and Cheyenne down along the Rosebud at the time, unaware that those self-same hostiles had already found him. The minute Crook had called a halt, they'd struck — and for the next six hours two groups of men, each a thousand-some strong, had found themselves locked in mortal combat.

Towards the end of it, one of the

Cheyenne jumped Tom and took his right arm off just above the elbow with a steel-headed tammix — what whites knew better as a tomahawk. Even so, Tom still managed to empty his pistol into the Indian's face before allowing himself to collapse.

A lesser man would have died from the shock alone. And a couple of times, after the Indians had been driven from the field and the surgeon-major finally got the chance to staunch the flow of blood and set about patching him back up, Tom came close to doing just that. But that was the thing about Tom Grandee — he was too mean even to die. With his one good hand he'd clung to life and slowly, inexorably clawed his way free of Death's long shadow. The only trouble was, the man who came back from the Rosebud in the June of '76 was even meaner than he had been before; even more unstable, unpredictable, and more likely than ever to explode at the slightest provocation.

O'Brien waited for him to explode

now. He didn't think there would be any dialogue. Tom would yell his brother's name, perhaps, and then his left hand — the hand he'd trained to be as fast if not faster than the one he'd lost, when it came to slapping leather — would swoop crosswise for the .44 and suddenly it would be kill or be killed all over again.

But all Tom said was, 'Hear tell you found yourself a fat Mexican woman an' settled down someplace around Nacozari.'

O'Brien inclined one shoulder. 'So they keep telling me.'

One of Tom's two companions, the other rangeman, chose that moment to speak up. 'O'Brien,' he murmured thoughtfully, and the way he said it made it sound like he was savouring the name.

Although he'd never seen the man before, O'Brien had seen the type more times than he could count. A two-gun man who wore his matched Peacemakers in crossed cartridge belts, their pockets tied low so that his palms would brush their grips with every swaggering step he took. A confident man, you'd think — over-confident, if anything — until you looked a little closer. Then you'd see a man who was anything *but* confident: a man with something to prove, and an overwhelming ache within him to prove it at any opportunity.

'Should I know you?' the man asked.

O'Brien shook his head. 'I don't think so.'

'This here's Wade Langham,' growled Tom in his low, measured rasp.

Langham was about thirty or so: a big, powerful man with a broad chest that pushed at the stitching of his grey percale shirt. He had a square, sunned face, a strong, well-defined jaw, cool brown eyes set deep into his head and a long, straight nose that arrowed down to a wide mouth. The mouth had some kind of kink in it that gave its owner a weird, secret smile he would never lose, not even at the moment of death, and

O'Brien found it as disturbing as hell.

'Langham,' he said.

Langham's only response was to very deliberately tilt his head sideways, first one way, then the other, to make the bones in his neck crack softly.

'Wade's my *segundo*,' Tom explained. 'An' this jasper here is my, uh, business associate, Lew Glass.'

Glass. Lyn Merrick had mentioned the name earlier. She'd been about to call him a mangy something-or-other when Rae Caulder had interrupted her.

Remembering that, O'Brien eyed the little man with fresh interest — not that he amounted to much. Glass was fifty or thereabouts, a shade below average height and tending some toward the gut. He had a pale, sweaty, humourless face and the restless eyes of a hunted animal. His jowls were clean-shaven, and beneath his narrow-brimmed grey hat it looked as if he wore his fair-to-red hair short and oiled. As he reached up and tugged nervously at his string tie, he mumbled something about being

81

pleased to make O'Brien's acquaintance, but he was a lousy liar.

'What brings you to Elkhorn?' asked Tom.

O'Brien looked back at him. He still couldn't decide whether or not Tom had heard about Al yet. If he had, he was taking the news awful well . . . and that wasn't like Tom at all. 'Whiskey,' he replied vaguely. 'A chance to sleep on something softer than ground. A decent meal.'

'You ought to try Quinlan's,' said Tom, his voice a low, chafing kind of sound. 'Damn' good eatery. Used to do a mighty fine steak at Quinlan's . . . 'fore we had to kill all the cattle, o' course.' He hooked his thumb over his shoulder. 'Come on. I'll walk you down there.'

'No need. I'll find it.'

'I'll walk you down there,' Tom repeated, his tone hardening noticeably. To his companions he said, 'I'll be back directly.'

After that, he and O'Brien pushed

out onto the street, O'Brien still half-expecting his unwelcome escort to make a move against him. But Tom merely gestured that they should turn right along Main, which they did, and for a while thereafter, the only sound was that of their boots on the plankwalk, and the soft, discordant jangle of Tom's spurs.

At last, glancing at O'Brien's profile, the one-armed man said, 'Lookin' for work?'

'Just passing through, is all.'

'That's as well. There *ain't* no work, leastways not in these parts. You heard about the hoof-an'-mouth, I guess?'

'Some.'

'Well, it finished things here,' Tom growled bitterly. 'Cut the cattle business stone dead. An' jus' when I thought I'd set down roots, become a man o' means.'

'Too bad.'

Tom nodded absently. 'You ever seen what it can do, the disease?' he asked.

'I've seen it,' said O'Brien. 'It isn't pretty.'

That was an understatement.

Because it was so highly contagious, hoof-and-mouth could scythe through a territory faster than greased lightning, and in almost less time thaN it took to tell, pretty much any critter in its path — cattle, swine, deer, antelope — found itself condemned to a lingering death. Unable to eat for the pus-filled blisters around their mouths, unable to walk for the skin damage to their hoofs, udders and teats, all its victims could do was smack their lips endlessly in a vain attempt to loosen the strings of saliva that hung there in long, glutinous cords, and wait for the suffering to end.

Faced with such an aggressive infection, there wasn't a whole lot a man could do save slaughter his stock and burn the bodies, and watch his livelihood — what there'd been of it — go up in smoke. But even that wasn't the worst of it, because those cattle who survived the disease were left as little more than scrawny bags of bones. More dead than alive, they gave less and less milk, and any calves they were carrying had to be aborted; strictly enforced quarantine statutes saw to that: statutes that could and did remain in force for months if not a year or more, until the territory was declared disease-free again.

Without warning, Tom suddenly came to a halt. 'Remember my brother, Al?' he rasped.

Sucking in a breath, O'Brien thought *Here it comes*, and prepared to haul iron. 'I remember Al,' he replied slowly.

But Tom made no move towards his own weapon. He just said, 'We figured to settle hereabouts, him an' me. 'Course, that was a while ago, and it was good country then. Had big plans, me an' Al — till it all went sour on us.'

Suddenly he struck out, smashing his left fist into a nearby porch-post with such force that O'Brien winced. 'Damn the luck,' Tom whispered, his jagged, ill-kept teeth clamping hard.

A long twenty seconds passed before he glanced down at his hand and saw with mild surprise that he'd split the knuckles. Slowly he brought them to his mouth so that he could taste the blood that came oozing to the surface like so many red pearls.

Watching him, O'Brien wondered if he should tell Tom what had become of his brother and take his chances. But even as he made to do just that, Grandee used his blood-smeared hand to gesture further along the street.

'There's Quinlan's,' he said. 'Get yourself fed, and then get yourself the hell outa this territory. There's nothing here for you, save misery.'

O'Brien nodded. 'I'll remember that.'

'Make sure you do,' grated Tom, and all at once there was nothing even remotely sociable left in him. He was all rattles now — cold and flat, mean and deadly. 'I got nothin' agin you, O'Brien,' he rasped. 'Hardly even *know* you, when it boils down to it. But I know what you *are*. You're a hired gun. An' you showin' up here, in *this* town, at *this* time . . . that irks me considerable.'

O'Brien's eyes narrowed. 'Why should it do that?' he asked innocently.

''Cause I've had my share o' trouble these past few months, an' I don't aim to have no more of it,' Tom spat in reply, giving his hand an impatient flick to rid it of the last of the blood. 'Now, mayhaps you *are* jus' passin' through, like you say. But if you're *not*, if you've been hired to come in here an' use that gun o' yourn — '

'I haven't.'

'Then we got no quarrel, have we?' countered Tom. 'Still, I'm a cautious man. I don't take risks, iffen I can help it. So here's what we'll do. First light tomorrow, you get the hell out of Elkhorn an' don't come back, 'cause if you *do*, me an' you might jus' get to buttin' heads. An' you won't like that, O'Brien. My word on it.'

O'Brien responded with a thin smile of his own. 'Go easy, Tom,' he advised. 'You might not find it all that pleasant yourself.'

A muscle in Tom's pale face twitched

briefly. 'Well, you been warned,' he growled. 'Show some sense an' *stay* warned. You'll live a whole heap longer if you do.'

And with that, he turned on his heel and started back the way he'd come, leaving O'Brien to watch him go and wonder just what in hell that little exchange had really been about. Something involving Jane Farrow and her sister, that much was certain. But *what*? And where did Caulder — *Doctor* Caulder, that was — fit into it all?

Unable to answer either question, he shook his head and turned towards the restaurant. But with memories of the hoof-and-mouth still clear in his mind — as well as the sure and certain knowledge that he was going to end up locking horns with Tom Grandee whether he wanted to or not — he realized that his appetite had temporarily deserted him.

4

He woke a little before daybreak the following morning, washed, shaved, gathered his belongings and then quit the dingy hotel room he'd booked into following his confrontation with Tom Grandee. The minute he stepped out onto the near-empty street, however, with the shadows of its clapboard buildings thrown long and deep across the hardpan by the slowly-rising sun, a voice off to his left said, 'Mornin'.'

O'Brien glanced around. Tom's *segundo*, Wade Langham, was lounging in an old hardwood chair a few yards away, arms folded across his broad chest, long legs shoved out ahead of him and crossed at the ankles. An insolent grin was making the kink in his lips do weird things and, as he climbed slowly to his feet, the challenge in his dark, deep-set eyes was impossible to miss.

'You're up early,' O'Brien observed.

Langham reached up to nudge his dark, high-crowned hat back off his tanned forehead. 'Early bird's the one that catches the worm,' he replied, tilting his head first one way, then the other, to make the bones there crack. Hooking his thumbs into his crossed cartridge belts, he used his square, clean-shaven jaw to indicate the warbag on O'Brien's shoulder. 'Quittin' town?' he asked.

'Looks that way.'

'Wise move. They's nothin' for you here save — '

' — misery,' finished O'Brien. 'You're too late, Langham. I've already had that particular speech from Tom.'

That made Langham's buckled smile widen a notch. 'An' I bet you just hated it, di'n't you?' he goaded. 'Bein' told to clear the county?'

O'Brien shrugged. 'Show me a man who wouldn't.'

'But you're goin' anyway,' Langham prodded.

'I wasn't aiming to stay.'

'Sure, sure.'

O'Brien couldn't help it: he snorted at the other man's clumsy attempts to provoke him, then said, 'See you around, Wade.'

'Maybe you will, at that,' Langham agreed, raising his voice as O'Brien stepped down into the street and started walking away from him. 'You ever show your face around here again, you can make *book* on it.'

Not bothering to look back, O'Brien went over to the livery to claim his horse. There was no sign of the stableman when he let himself inside — it was still too early — so he led the blood-bay from its stall, checked the animal's bruised shoulder briefly, satisfied himself that it was healing nicely, then set about saddling up in silence.

He supposed he should have felt flattered that Tom had sent Langham to make sure he left town, but he felt more irritated than anything else. It didn't sit well with him to back down from any man, especially a man like Langham, who could stand to have some of the vinegar knocked out of him. And yet another confrontation would have served no real purpose, save to get one or both of them injured or worse.

Still, he was damned if he'd quit town like a whipped dog. No — it might sound foolish, but the least he could do was go in his own time, and at his own pace. Besides which, the appetite that had deserted him the night before had returned with a vengeance this morning, and he didn't aim to go anywhere without taking the pleats out of his belly first.

By the time he led the horse out onto the street, the sun had climbed a little higher and the shadows had retreated a touch. Langham, he saw, had gone back to lounging in the hardwood chair. He stepped up to leather and walked the animal past the hotel and on up towards Quinlan's, feeling Langham's eyes following him every yard of the way. He dismounted outside the eatery, threw a hitch at the rail and went inside to order breakfast.

Business looked to be as bad here as it was all over town, and apart from a sleepy-eyed waitress who was hovering in a curtained doorway at the back of the premises, the restaurant was deserted. The woman waited until he'd settled himself at a small corner table with his back to the wall and a good view of the street beyond the dusty, half-curtained window, then came to take his order.

He didn't have to wait long for it to arrive, and was just forking up the last of his eggs when another rider drew rein outside. As he drained his coffee cup, he watched the newcomer swing down, tie a small paint horse to the rail beside his and then come inside.

It was Lyn Merrick.

She hesitated a moment in the doorway, looking around until she saw him dabbing at his mouth with a bunched napkin. Then, drawing down a heavy breath that did some very interesting things to the front of her grey placket shirt and the dark box jacket she wore over it, she finally closed the door behind her and came across to him.

'Spotted your horse outside,' she said by way of greeting. 'Mind if I sit down a while?'

'Help yourself,' he told her. 'Coffee?'

'No, thanks.' Taking off her wide-brimmed hat, the girl sat with her small, tough-looking hands clasped on the table in front of her. 'I was hopin' I'd catch you before you left town,' she said without noticeable conviction. 'I, ah . . . well, could be I owe you an apology. What I said yesterday, I said in the heat of the moment, an' if I offended you, I'm sorry.'

'You sure *sound* sorry,' O'Brien noted with heavy sarcasm.

Immediately she bristled, as he'd known she would. 'Well, take it whichever way you choose,' she snapped, hostility flaring briefly in her hazel eyes. 'That makes no nevermind to me. But if you're still in the market for a job . . . ?'

Common sense dictated that he say no, he wasn't, and be done with it. There was something going on in these parts that was likely to blow sky-high at any moment, and a wise man would be someplace else when the explosion finally occurred. But the more he was pushed, the more O'Brien tended to dig in and stand his ground — and between them, Tom Grandee and Wade Langham had done all the pushing he was prepared to allow. Besides which, he was still more than a mite curious about just what that aforementioned *something* might be.

'Well, that depends on the job,' he said at last. 'And why the change of heart.'

She shrugged, the movement sending a shimmer of light and colour through her long auburn hair, and when she replied, she was careful to keep her voice low. 'The job, I really can't say, not yet, and certainly not here. But if things shake out the way we expect them to, it could be that you'll need to use that gun of yours some more.'

He laughed briefly. 'That tells me a lot.'

'It tells you as much as you're likely to get right now,' she replied, biting off every word. 'As for the change of heart, well, that's easier to understand. Rae Caulder won't work for us unless we guarantee his safety. The only way we can do that is to give him back his precious bodyguard — *you*.'

'So without me . . . ?'

'We don't get Caulder,' she explained. 'Well — are you interested or not?'

'I'm interested,' he replied, telling himself he was a blame' fool.

'Then let's get moving,' said Lyn, rising. 'I don't like to be away from the ranch too long. 'Sides, the sooner we get home, the sooner you find out just what it is you're signing on for.'

'Ma'am,' he said with feeling, 'I can hardly wait.'

* * *

Lyn Merrick might not have been too happy to have him around, but Rae Caulder greeted him like a pup with two tails.

'Mr O'Brien!' he called, as they drew rein and dismounted in front of the ranch house, 'I'm glad to see you again, sir — more glad than you can know.'

Jane Farrow had followed him out onto the veranda, the red-headed boy at her side. As O'Brien glanced across at her, she offered him that tremulous little smile of hers and said, 'Thank you for coming back, Mr O'Brien. I trust we'll show you a sight more hospitality today.'

'I sure hope so, ma'am.'

The boy, whose round-eyed, unblinking stare showed just how fascinated he was by O'Brien, suddenly tugged at Jane's long brown skirt to get her attention. When he had it, he went up onto his toes so that he could whisper something in her ear. At the end of it she smiled, nodded and said, 'Yes, Clay — he's a friend.'

'Well, we *hope* he's a friend,' Lyn amended sourly.

The boy, Clay, studied O'Brien some more. He was a shade taller than his ten years, and he had Jane's same green eyes and a button nose that was splashed with freckles. At last, he said shyly, 'Howdy, mister.'

'Howdy back,' said O'Brien. 'Your boy, ma'am?'

'My boy,' Jane replied, adding with quiet pride, 'Clay Farrow Junior.'

'An' I'm Spark,' called a new voice. 'Abel Spark.'

O'Brien turned just as the whiskery old man who'd been skulking around the barn the day before, keeping him and Caulder covered with a Burnside carbine that looked as old and ill-used as the grease-stained cardigan shirt that covered his sunken chest, came shuffling across the yard to take their reins. He wiped his free hand on the front of the shirt, then thrust it forward. 'Mornin' to yuh,' he said in a high, brisk voice. 'I work for these good people, cook for their crew — when they *got* a crew, that is. So you keep on my good side, lessen you wanna go hungry, y'hear?'

Spark was well on in years, and looked it. His skin had been baked by more than sixty summers and scored through by what appeared to be a million wrinkles. His eyes were blue and rheumy, his nose a long, pitted beak that overhung a straight, thin-lipped mouth. He was a shade below six feet in height, thin as a rail and bald but for a fine scraping of feathery white hair that refused to lie flat against his skull.

'Abel's more than a cook,' said Lyn, and for the first time her tough, no-nonsense manner seemed to melt a little as she regarded the old man. 'He's more like one o' the family.'

Spark offered her a mocking glance.

'Aw, shucks, Missy Lyn,' he teased, deadpan, 'you'll set me to blushin' if you ain't careful.'

O'Brien shook hands with him and was impressed by the old man's firm grip. The feeling must have been mutual, because Spark gave him a nod, almost of approval, before calling to Clay, 'How 'bout you givin' me a hand with these here hosses, young 'un?'

As they led the horses away, Jane said, 'Come on inside, and we'll get down to cases.'

He, Lyn and Caulder followed her into a long, plain room with a low ceiling. At the far end sat a cast-iron Franklin stove, a sawbuck table, a pie safe and some shelves filled with airtights and sacks of flour. At the other stood an imposing rock fireplace around which had been arranged an ancient sofa and some rawhide chairs. A small harmonium occupied one corner, on top of which sat a framed daguerreotype of a sandy-haired man aged about forty. This, O'Brien guessed, was Clay Farrow Senior.

As they took seats at the sawbuck table, Jane asked, 'Has, uh, Lyn told you why we asked you back?'

'I didn't tell him any more than I had to,' Lyn cut in.

'Then I'd best begin at the beginning,' Jane decided, pausing briefly to order her thoughts. 'You've heard about the hoof-and-mouth, of course.'

'Ma'am, that seems to be *all* I've heard about lately.'

'Well, it's the hoof-and-mouth that's at the heart of this business, Mr O'Brien. But it could be that I'm getting a little ahead of myself.

'For many years,' she continued, 'our nearest neighbour was a man named Jim Glass. Jim's spread, the Circle G, is the biggest outfit in these parts, and Jim ran it with a will of iron. He was a hard man, and he surrounded himself with equally hard men, whose job it was to ... well, let's say to 'protect his interests'. The hardest of those men was and remains a gunslinger by the name of Tom Grandee.'

'We've met,' said O'Brien.

'Then you'll know just how thoroughly disagreeable a man Tom Grandee is,' Jane replied. 'To all intents and purposes, he was Jim's foreman, but Jim really kept him around to handle all the less than legal chores that needed tending. He was well paid for the work too — if you can call it work — but after a time he started to get ideas above his station. Eventually it got so that he didn't want to be the hired man anymore, he wanted to be the man who did the hiring — an equal partner in Circle G.'

'How did Glass take that?'

Jane snorted. 'Well, the very notion was ridiculous, of course, and he told Grandee as much.'

'An' *that*,' murmured Lyn, 'is why Jim died.'

O'Brien frowned at her. 'Tom killed him?'

She nodded. 'Not that anyone could

prove it, o' course. But he did it, all right.'

'What happened?'

She pursed her lips. 'Jim was a drinking man. They say he got drunk one night, took a tumble an' knocked over a lantern. The short of it is, there was a fire, and Jim died. County coroner called it death by misadventure, but the talk in these parts is that Tom clubbed Jim senseless when they got to arguin', which they was doin' all the time towards the end, then started the fire deliberately, to finish him off.'

'His thinking,' said Jane, picking up the story. 'was that when Jim's brother Lew inherited the ranch, he'd be a sight easier to handle than Jim ever was.'

'And *was* he?' asked O'Brien, already knowing the answer.

'Lew never did have any backbone,' Lyn supplied venomously. 'An' after what happened to Jim, he was so scared of Tom an' his brother that he let 'em move in an' run the ranch like it was their own.'

'So Tom finally got what he wanted,' said Jane. 'But just when him and Al more or less took over the Circle G — '

' — along came the hoof-and-mouth,' guessed O'Brien.

Jane nodded. 'He lost 'most everything, up to and including a lucrative government contract to supply beef to the Ute Indians down at the White River Agency,' she confirmed. Then, with a fleeting glance at her sister, she added softly, 'And that's where we come in.'

Sensing that they were finally getting to the point, O'Brien looked at her with fresh interest. Jane explained, 'Jim's agreement with the government stipulates that if for any reason he is unable to fulfil the contract, another supplier can step in to replace him.' She squared her broad shoulders and said, 'I intend to be that supplier.'

He frowned. 'But there's no beef to be had in these parts.'

The pout of her lips suddenly gave way to a smile, and there was nothing tremulous about it this time. 'That's where you're wrong, Mr O'Brien,' she told him. 'I have a herd of approximately one hundred-and-fifty head hidden away in the hills — and, what's more, they're free of disease and ready for delivery.'

★   ★   ★

O'Brien sat up straight and asked, 'How the *heck* did you manage that?'

He'd addressed the question to Jane, but it was Rae Caulder who replied. 'Oh, they're not *immune*, if that's what you're thinking,' he said. 'It's simply that the herd has apparently been kept in isolation for the better part of a year. The hoof-and-mouth just . . . passed them by.'

O'Brien turned to him. 'And where do *you* fit into all this?

'I'm a veterinarian,' said the greenhorn, confirming what O'Brien had already guessed. 'Mrs Farrow hired me to inspect her herd and ensure that they are indeed free of disease, as she claims. As you are doubtless aware, quarantine laws state that no stock may be moved, much less offered for sale, until it has been declared healthy. I have the authority to make that declaration.'

'Wouldn't your local vet have done just as well, Mrs Farrow?'

'Certainly,' she agreed. 'But our local man is in Tom Grandee's pocket. He'd have blocked us any way he could, if it meant keeping us from winning that contract, and at the end of it he'd have more than likely betrayed the location of the herd to Grandee. Then Tom could have waltzed right in there and helped himself.'

'They're hidden away, then?'

'Up in the hills,' Jane replied, nodding, 'and about as safe as they can be.'

'You're sure about that?'

'We're sure,' said Lyn. 'It's like a maze up there, all draws, breaks an' canyons. Lessen you know where to look, you'd never find 'em.'

'But Tom got to hear about them.'

'It was never going to stay a secret forever,' Jane sighed. 'And when we finally decided to call in Dr Caulder, the word got out and Tom put two and two together. He came here and tried to bully me into selling him the herd, sight unseen, but I told him they weren't for sale, especially not for the pittance he was offering.'

'What did he say to that?'

'He told me I'd regret my decision, although he hasn't made any kind of move against me yet. But as you know, he *did* send his brother and this other man, George Weedon, to make sure that Dr Caulder never made it to Elkhorn.'

She sat forward, her hands suddenly clasping with enough force to leech the blood from her knuckles. 'Still, he's a desperate man, Mr O'Brien. And with the market being the way it is right now, he knows that my herd will fetch top dollar. That money could help him survive an otherwise ruinous year, and enable him to build a new herd from scratch. More than that, it would ensure that he keeps the White River contract — and that is something I am not prepared to countenance.'

'Why not?'

'I owe it to my husband,' Jane replied, drawing herself up again. 'He worked tirelessly to build the Long Branch herd — indeed, you could say that he worked himself to a premature death. He started with practically nothing, and was told every step of the way that he was crazy, just a dreamer who would never achieve his goal. But that only made him all the more determined to succeed. And so he put every ounce of his considerable knowledge into devising a breeding programme that would prove his detractors wrong. And all through those long years of trial and error, of disappointment and the occasional triumph, his ambition remained the same — to one day take over the White River contract, supply his beef to the Indians and, in so doing, revolutionize the cattle industry.'

At last she came up for air. 'Sadly,' she concluded, 'he died before he could make that happen. And so it falls to me to finish what he started.'

O'Brien sat back again, the chair beneath him creaking softly. There it was, then. The only disease-free herd to be had for at least 200 miles in any direction, if Jane Farrow was to be believed, and worth a king's ransom because of it. For Jane it meant some sort of validation; for Grandee it meant survival. And here he was, being asked to plant himself right between the two of them and in all likelihood get his fool head blown off.

'So you want me to ride shotgun on Caulder here, till he can satisfy himself that your herd's fit to be offered for sale,' he said.

'Yes. And to help protect us against Tom Grandee, of course, should the need arise.'

O'Brien smiled briefly. 'That might not be so easy, Mrs Farrow. If Grandee does decide to come here with blood in his eyes, he'll fetch a crew of gunnies to back him, and there won't be much I can do against a whole pack of 'em.'

'Look,' snapped Lyn, 'all we're askin' is that you stick around, keep your eyes skinned an' do whatever you can to keep Grandee off our backs long enough for Caulder here to examine the herd an' give 'em a clean bill of health. Once he's satisfied that they're fit for sale, we can make our bid for the White River contract, an' that'll be an end to it.'

'You think so?' he countered. 'Mrs Farrow, you just said it yourself — Tom Grandee's desperate and disagreeable. If you put him out of business, it won't matter much to him that you're a woman, a mother, a widow — he'll do whatever it takes to make sure you go down with him.'

Before that could properly sink in, he hit them with another consideration. 'Suppose you get this contract, anyway. How do you figure to drive your herd down to the White River Agency without a crew?'

Lyn said defiantly, 'We'll find men, when the time comes.'

'Men willing to stand against the likes of Tom Grandee and Wade Langham? I doubt it.'

'We'll find men somewhere,' insisted Jane. 'And if we can't . . . '

Her voice trailed away.

He climbed slowly to his feet. Much as he hated to dishearten her, he'd heard enough. He'd known at the outset that this was a powder keg of a situation, of course, but he saw now that it was an impossible one, too, because what Jane Farrow was really proposing to do was push 150 head about eighty to a hundred miles south-west with nothing more than her sister, her son and their cook.

Softening his tone, he began, 'Mrs Farrow, I'm sorry, but — '

'Please, Mr O'Brien,' she broke in. '*Please*. You don't know the full story yet. Perhaps when you see the herd, you'll understand why this is so important, not just for me or my husband, but . . . '

He looked into those gentle green eyes of hers and saw, behind them, a woman who was right on the edge. One more setback, one more disappointment, and she'd be finished for good, and they both knew it. So, soft-hearted sonofabitch that he was, he sighed and said, 'All right, ma'am. I don't see what difference it'll make, but what the heck, I'm here now — so let's go see this herd of yours.'

* * *

It took them a long three hours to reach their destination. Jane led the way aboard a leggy sorrel she rode side-saddle, and O'Brien, Lyn and Caulder followed on behind, holding their own mounts to a steady trot.

The redhead led them into the foothills behind the ranch house, then deeper into the high country beyond.

They passed between tall granite peaks and on through an immense, sweet-smelling pine grove. Sometimes the land turned rugged and uneven, sometimes it flattened out into lush tableland, but always there remained one constant — a heavy, eerie blanket of silence which, in turn, inspired an unshakeable sense of isolation.

As the morning wore on, O'Brien spotted the tracks of elk, black bear, fox and badger, but saw no other signs of life, either human or animal. They followed a steep-walled ravine for what seemed like forever, then charted a winding course through vast belts of Douglas fir and golden aspen. Sometimes they climbed higher, sometimes they had to descend into deep, shadowy hollows where the temperature dropped noticeably. They doubled back on themselves at least once, then pushed north-west across a wide boulder field, then south, then south-east and back again.

Shaking his head at the complexity of

it all, O'Brien told himself that Lyn hadn't been kidding when she'd described this high country as a maze. And as they pushed on across grey, shaly slopes stippled with sagebrush and drooping lungwort, he could only marvel at Jane's ability to navigate this web of trails and half-trails and no-trails-at-all and not get them hopelessly, helplessly lost.

A little after noon, she led them through one final belt of timber and out onto a rugged, grassy plateau sprinkled with wild flowers and the occasional shallow, grass-fringed waterhole. A few hundred yards further on, the land began to drop towards a long, mile-wide valley, its precipitous slopes fortified by well-weathered pines and Gambel oak, and it was here that Jane signed that they should all rein down.

As he crossed his arms over his saddle horn and stretched a little to ease the knots in his back and butt, O'Brien surveyed the basin to which she had brought them. Everything was so perfectly tranquil that it looked more like a painting than a scene from real life. Sunlight danced and sparkled on the breeze-ruffled surface of a small lake at its far end, and illuminated a small, crude line shack on its southern shore, which had long-since fallen into disrepair. The lake itself was surrounded by a belt of sedge, the sedge gradually yielding to a lusher, taller carpet of bluestem and grama grass, which swayed and rippled lazily in the warm zephyr. From the timber to the north-east came the persistent drilling of an industrious woodpecker, the easily recognizable sound set against the equally distinctive calls of ptarmigan, lark and magpie.

Then O'Brien looked a little closer at the animals spread out along the valley floor, grazing contentedly or bellowing to each other and, as he ranged his pale-blue eyes from one beast to the next, his eyebrows slowly drew together.

Something here wasn't quite *right*.

He didn't say anything immediately, just reached into his saddle-bags, took out his field-glasses and studied the animals more carefully.

They looked like cattle. *Looked* like. But they weren't like any cattle he'd ever seen before. They were . . . *bigger* somehow . . . chunkier, with heavier, humped shoulders, deeper chests and thicker legs, and there were longish tufts of hair hanging from their chins.

A long moment passed before he finally lowered the glasses and turned to Jane, who was sitting her horse beside him. 'Ma'am . . . ' he began, but words failed him and he had to start again. 'What the hell kind of herd is this, Mrs Farrow?'

Flashing him a smile of pure, proud triumph, Jane said, 'They're the future, Mr O'Brien. *This* is what's going to revolutionize the cattle business.'

5

'They're the offspring of a Hereford bull and buffalo cows,' she continued, 'and they are called 'cattalo'.'

Insects scythed and fluttered around him as he considered that. 'Is that . . . *natural*?' he enquired at length.

'It's not like trying to cross a cat with a dog, Mr O'Brien,' said Caulder, requesting the use of the field-glasses with one outstretched hand. 'Both the cow and the buffalo are from the same bovid family, after all. Neither is the idea a new or particularly *un*natural one. Crossbreeds were first seen more than a century ago, when the cow and the buffalo mated entirely of their own volition. Since then, the Canadians have tried breeding them. The rancher Charles Goodnight has bred them, crossing the buffalo — or bison, to give it its more correct nomenclature — not with Herefords, as Mrs Farrow's late husband did, but with Angus cattle. And a Kansan by the name of C.J. 'Buffalo' Jones is attempting to breed a herd even as we speak.'

O'Brien asked the obvious question. 'Why?'

'To create a hardier animal,' supplied Jane. 'And they're certainly that, Mr O'Brien. They have a thicker coat, as you may have noticed, which means they are better able to survive all but the harshest winters. They are also excellent foragers, showing as they do considerably more initiative than an ordinary cow. Their meat is leaner, too, and each animal gives more of it.'

O'Brien took another thoughtful look at the herd. Twenty years ago, more than fifty million buffalo had roamed this country. Now, only a fraction of that number remained. The white man had taken to killing them for a variety of reasons — for sport, for their hides, for their tongues, which were considered a delicacy back East. But he'd also slaughtered them in order to weaken the Indian, who relied on them for just about everything, from meat and tools to fuel and shelter.

To undo two decades of wholesale destruction and help bring something very much like the buffalo back into being . . .

Suddenly he began to appreciate Clay Farrow's dream a little better.

Just then a movement in the timber about 200 yards to the north-west caught his attention and, as he turned that way, two black-billed magpies took to the air with a heavy beating of wings. He watched them climb and wheel for a moment, his thoughts still elsewhere, and was just about to turn back to the herd when something else caught his eye — a pair of tuft-eared squirrels darting up the bole of an oak tree in roughly the same area.

He realized then that the woodpecker over that way had stopped his drilling, too.

'My congratulations, Mrs Farrow,'

Caulder was saying, still studying the herd through the field-glasses. 'This truly is a magnificent achievement.'

Ignoring the conversation, O'Brien kept his eyes on the ridge, watching, waiting. The timber along the rim was packed close and bordered by a wild jumble of mountain shrubs, blooming now in a mass of bright yellow flowers. Behind the trees and bushes lay only deep brown shadows sliced through by stray shafts of dusty half-light, and what little sunlight managed to penetrate the tangled boughs lay like scattered patches of molten gold on the forest floor beneath.

When a small cloud of bluebirds quit the timber a few seconds later, he decided that he'd seen enough. As he started to gather up his reins, Lyn asked, 'What is it?'

Low and with absolute certainty, he replied, 'Someone's over there, in those trees.'

Behind him, Jane drew in a sharp breath. Caulder said, '*What?*' and quickly swung the field-glasses that way.

Lyn snapped, 'What do we do?'

Backing the blood-bay away from them, O'Brien said grimly, 'Find out who it is.'

He turned his horse and started for the timber at a canter, hoping that the direct approach would flush out who-ever was over there. As luck would have it, he'd only gone a dozen yards or so when his quarry realized he'd been spotted and tried to make a break for it.

The first thing that gave him away was the muted drumming of his horse's hoofs, moving at speed. A moment later O'Brien spotted a vague blur of motion flitting between the distant trees, and irregular patches of sunlight spilling backwards off something grey that was headed east at a gallop.

Jaw clamping tight, he kicked his own mount to speed and sent it surging north-east across the plateau, figuring to intercept the rider before he could show them a clean pair of heels. Moments later the blood-bay veered east, onto a course that paralleled the timberline, and now O'Brien could just about see the man he was after, in among all the shadows, no more than twenty yards to his left and about twice that distance ahead. The man's horse was weaving to right and left to keep from running into trees or stumbling over deadfalls, and the man himself was constantly having to dodge this way and that to avoid colliding with low-hanging branches.

Out in the open and not burdened by the same hazards, O'Brien slowly but surely started to gain on him, and chancing a quick glance around, his quarry saw as much and decided that he'd make better time if *he* quit the timber as well.

Seconds later he did just that. His horse swerved to the right and burst out of the trees, still the better part of thirty yards ahead. The horse, O'Brien noted, was a muscular charcoal and it was going flat-out, the rider himself still crouched low in the saddle, his long legs working furiously as he raked spur-hung heels along the animal's flanks to make it go even faster.

O'Brien saw a dark, high-crowned hat, a pale-grey shirt and broad shoulders, and thought with a curse, *Langham*.

The sonofabitch must have followed him and Lyn out from town, and then managed to trail them right to the valley Jane and Lyn had been so confident no one would ever find, save maybe by accident.

He swore again for having let it happen, and slapped the split reins back and forth across the blood-bay's heaving neck to urge his own mount to greater speed. If Langham got away and told Grandee where he'd find the cattle he needed so badly, Jane's plan — Jane's *dream* — was finished for good, and he couldn't allow that to happen.

Langham suddenly hipped around and chanced another look behind him. With amazing clarity, O'Brien saw the deep set of his cool brown eyes, the line of his long, straight nose, the peculiar twist of his wide mouth. A moment later, Langham pulled his right-side Peacemaker, jabbed his arm back and pulled the trigger.

Flame lanced from the short-barrelled weapon a fraction ahead of the malicious snap of the shot itself, and O'Brien called the other man seven kinds of bastard for being so damn' trigger-happy.

Then, right out of the blue, Langham's charcoal ran straight into one of the shallow waterholes with which the plateau was riddled, and which, until you were right on top of them, were rendered all but invisible by the tall, shaggy grass with which they were surrounded.

The animal plunged belly-deep into the scummy water and almost collapsed there and then, but somehow kept its balance, managed to recover and half-lurched, half-threw itself toward the far bank.

Water exploded around its thrusting

hoofs as it pitched forward, with Langham rocking perilously back and forth in the saddle, his pants and boots soaked through. Moments later the charcoal vaulted up onto dry land again, but it was spooked now, and made clumsy because of it.

Again the animal stumbled, its wet hoofs failing to find purchase on the sodden grass. It slewed sideways, and Langham, still turned half-around in the saddle, trying to line up another shot, was suddenly flung from the horse's back.

He slammed hard against the ground and rolled two or three yards, the Peacemaker flying from his grasp. As his wall-eyed mount staggered back up and continued to run O'Brien, coming in fast, brought the blood-bay to a halt no more than twelve feet away.

He came down off the horse so fast it was more like a fall than a dismount, but Langham, hatless now, was already climbing back to his feet, his movements unsteady, his weird smile rucked into a grimace.

Planting himself, he clawed for his left-side Peacemaker, swept it out fast and loosed off a shot, but the fall had played hell with his co-ordination and because he triggered too soon, the shot ploughed into the ground.

Not waiting for him to try his luck again, O'Brien bulled in, ripped the gun from his fingers and punched him in the face.

Langham staggered and went down onto one knee, a line of blood coursing down his chin from a split in his lower lip. He glared back at O'Brien, and O'Brien saw that look in his eyes again, that mixture of self-doubt coupled with an almost uncontainable need to prove himself at every opportunity.

Tossing the gun into the waterhole, he growled, 'Forget it, Langham.'

But Langham had other ideas. Giving vent to a sound that was part-roar, part-scream, he suddenly rushed O'Brien, caught him around the middle and drove him back until they both slammed into the waiting blood-bay. The animal whickered and shied away, and both men went down in a tangle, Langham on top, still roaring, trying to hold O'Brien's shoulders flat to the ground with his wet knees so that he could use his fists on his face. O'Brien wasn't having that, though. With a twist he unseated his opponent, sent him flying over on to his side, and then they rolled away from each other, leapt back to their feet, and now each man had his fists balled and ready, his shoulders hunched, his guard up.

Langham came in and threw a right. O'Brien blocked it, jabbed a short punch of his own into Langham's exposed ribs, heard the man grunt, smelled the foul breath that gusted from his crooked mouth. Batting Langham's right arm aside, he hit him again, in the stomach this time, then followed with a right cross, a left to the ribs, another right to the stomach.

Langham staggered under the force

of the blows, then lunged forward and tried to kick him in the groin. O'Brien danced back, caught his leg 'twixt knee and ankle, twisted hard and sent Langham crashing back to the ground, where he squirmed through the tall grass like the oversized rattlesnake he was.

'Give it up, Langham,' O'Brien growled, breathing hard. 'You're finished.'

That, however, was a view Langham refused to share. Stubbornly, gasping for air, he pushed up onto all fours, his splayed hands hidden by the tall grass. 'Think . . . so?' he wheezed.

In the next instant, he twisted around and powered back to his feet, and O'Brien saw, too late, that he had a gun in his right fist — the Peacemaker he'd dropped when he'd fallen from his horse, and which he must have blundered across during all his squirming.

Even as he brought the weapon up, O'Brien threw himself forward, rammed him backwards with one hunched shoulder, then grabbed his gun-hand by the wrist and thrust it skyward. Langham tried to tilt the weapon so that he could put a bullet through the top of O'Brien's skull, but that was something else O'Brien wasn't about to allow. Teeth grinding, he squeezed Langham's wrist so hard that the bones very nearly splintered, and with no real choice in the matter, Langham howled and had to drop the weapon a second time.

Fighting mad now, he stamped down on O'Brien's right foot, then tore his gun-hand free and swung a roundhouse right that caught O'Brien on the left ear. Pain flared hotly, and then that side of his face went numb and suddenly the only thing he could hear was the thin, protesting whine of his battered eardrum.

Langham came steaming back in, fists bunched and hammering, but O'Brien, suddenly as calm as Langham was crazy, hooked a fist deep into his belly, another, a right cross, a left, a right, a left, and suddenly the blows started coming so hard and so fast that there wasn't a single damn' thing Langham could do to stop them.

He lumbered backwards in a vain attempt to escape the barrage, but his legs were already giving way beneath him and his guard was rapidly turning into an ineffectual flailing of arms.

In any case, O'Brien wasn't about to let him go *anywhere*, not now. He dished out one more right cross, one more left, and Langham's head snapped one way, then the other. Back he went, his retreat more of a drunken lurch than anything else, but still O'Brien went after him, punching, jabbing, taking no pleasure in it but knowing it had to be done.

And then, at last, Langham's eyes rolled back in his head, and O'Brien knew, with no small relief, that it was over.

Langham collapsed in a heap at his feet.

O'Brien stood over him for a moment or two, swaying slightly, breathing hard, fists still balled, waiting for him to move again.

He didn't.

Finally, he sleeved his sweat-streaked face, checked his teeth with his tongue, then bent to retrieve his hat, which he'd lost sometime during the fight. That done, he flopped down beside the waterhole and did what he could to clean himself up.

His head was pounding fit to bust, but the cool water helped to clear it a little. A new thought occurred to him, and he shoved back to his feet, stumbled back to Langham, turned him over with the tip of one boot and checked through his pockets. A moment later he discovered a stub of pencil and a scrap of paper upon which a series of letters and numbers had been inexpertly scrawled. His lips compressed as he read the first line.

W7 NW13 S4 SE9 S6.

The sound of approaching horses told him that Jane, Lyn and Caulder had finally decided to put in an appearance. As they reined down nearby, Jane took one look at his face and said, 'Mr O'Brien! My God, are you all right?'

He nodded tiredly.

Lyn, however, was more interested in Langham. 'He followed us from town,' she guessed.

'I reckon.'

'And now he knows where the herd's hidden,' added Jane.

O'Brien looked at her. 'Maybe.'

'What does that mean?'

He held up the scrap of paper. 'I just found this in Langham's pocket. It's a map, of sorts. Looks to me like he was keeping a rough tally of miles and points of the compass to make sure he could find the place again.'

Jane's expression suddenly slackened as she realized what he was saying. 'So if we were to destroy those directions . . . ' she began hopefully.

O'Brien nodded. 'He'd stand no more chance of finding his way back up here than he did at first light this morning. Still, we can't take that for granted. I spotted plenty of landmarks on the way up here. Could be Langham did, too. And even the smallest detail could still point him in the right direction, should he try and retrace his steps.' He thought for a moment, then said, 'Can you find another spot to hold the herd? Just to be on the safe side?'

'Nothing as good.'

'It only has to be long enough for Caulder to carry out his tests — and keep Tom Grandee off your back.'

'There's a high meadow about ten miles from here,' Lyn suggested. 'They'd be safe there, I reckon.'

'We'll move 'em, then,' O'Brien proposed, though rounding up and driving cattle — *cattalo*, he corrected himself — was the last thing he felt like doing just then.

'All right,' Jane agreed. 'But what about Langham?'

'He's not apt to cause us any more trouble for a while, but I'll tie him to a tree and we'll collect him when we're finished here.'

'After that, I mean.'

O'Brien shrugged. 'There's not a whole lot we *can* do, save take him back to the ranch and turn him loose.'

'Turn him — !' Lyn repeasted. 'That's beggin' for trouble, O'Brien. Wade Langham's not the kind of gent who turns the other cheek, you know. He'll want blood for what you did to him today.'

'I guess he will, at that,' O'Brien replied with a sigh. 'But it's going to come to shooting between him and me sooner or later, anyway, and unfortunately the same goes for Tom Grandee. Best I can hope for right now is to make it later, rather than sooner.'

★   ★   ★

It was well past suppertime when they eventually got back to the ranch.

Clay, who'd been anxiously awaiting the return of his mother all afternoon, spotted them immediately, and made a chicken-scattering dash across the yard and into the cookshack to report their arrival to Abel Spark. A few moments later the old-timer came shuffling through the doorway with the boy at his side, pointing excitedly.

Spark put one bony, flour-whitened hand up to shield his eyes from the last of the day's glare, and his whiskery mouth worked silently as he watched them come down from the foothills and on across the flats.

Jane came first, he saw, holding her sweated horse to a weary walk. Missy Lyn followed on behind and to one side of her. Then came the vet, Caulder, and then the new man, O'Brien.

But O'Brien was leading a fifth animal, a charcoal horse, astride which was slumped another man.

The old cook's liquid blue eyes closed down a notch when he recognized Wade Langham, and his frown deepened still further when he saw how lifeless the man appeared, his shoulders slack, his chin resting on his chest.

'Trouble?' Spark enquired, when they finally drew rein outside the barn, and

Clay hurried forward to take his mother's reins.

With a tired nod, Jane slipped down from her saddle, gave the boy a hug and briefly told the cook what had happened.

After O'Brien had roped Langham to a tree, rounded up the man's horse and left it picketed nearby, he, Jane, Lyn and Caulder, riding flank, swing, point and drag respectively, had set about driving Jane's herd to the pasture Lyn had suggested. O'Brien had been a mite chary of the cattalo at first, not knowing what to expect from them, but they'd proven to be of placid disposition and relatively easy to move. Still, it had taken them a fair while to reach the new bed-ground, and the day was waning fast by the time they'd come back for Tom Grandee's *segundo*.

Langham had regained consciousness while they were gone, but only just. When O'Brien untied him and dragged him to his feet, he'd swung an instinctive but sloppy punch that

O'Brien had no trouble dodging, then promptly collapsed in a muttering heap. With a sigh, O'Brien had hauled him back up and somehow got him settled into his saddle, and after shoving his boots into the stirrups and ensuring that he was reasonably well balanced, they'd begun the long, roundabout ride back to the ranch.

As one mile followed another, Langham had continued to drift in and out of consciousness and mutter venomously under his breath, but O'Brien doubted that he really knew where he was or remembered for sure just what had happened to him. Neither did all the bouncing around he suffered on the difficult return journey do much to improve his condition.

Now, O'Brien handed his reins and those of the charcoal to Clay and reached up to get Langham down. 'You might have to give me a hand with this one, Mr Spark,' he said, wincing at the pain in his punished joints.

The old man frowned. 'He's *stayin?*'

'I don't like it any more'n you do, Abel,' said Lyn. 'But he's not in any fit state to ride on. O'Brien thinks he might have a couple of busted ribs.'

'Hmmm,' Spark allowed, giving Langham a quick appraisal. 'Could be concussed, too. I seen it before, an' he's got the look.'

As he helped O'Brien half-slide, half-pull Langham out of his saddle, he decided, 'We'll get him bedded down in the bunkhouse, an' then I'll see what I can do to patch him up.'

'You jus' try it . . . ' Langham husked, the words raspy and distorted by his swollen lips.

'Aw, button it, mister,' Spark retorted. 'I got no time for you, nor the low comp'ny you keep. But I've never yet turned my back on a man as needed tendin' — not even a maggot like you. So you jus' set all your fightin' talk aside an' let ol' Abel fix you up, y'hear?'

Between them, he and O'Brien drag-walked Langham into the bunkhouse and stretched him out, none too gently, on the nearest cot. Langham didn't put up much of a struggle, but continued to mumble threats the whole time.

'I thought I told you to stow all that fightin' talk?' said Spark, thumbing back Langham's eyelids and inspecting his pupils for signs of internal bleeding. Over his shoulder he said to O'Brien, 'Best you go get yourself cleaned up, son. I'll tend to this jasper's ailments, then fix you all some eats.'

'Appreciate it, Mr Spark.'

'Oh, an' another thing. My given name's Abel. Be proud iffen you'd use it.'

'Thanks. I will.'

He went back outside, still aching like hell. There was no sign of Lyn or Caulder, but Jane was watching her son as he struggled to off-saddle the salt-stained horses and turn them out into one of the two corrals so that they could roll, drink, socialize, or all three. The boy was finding it difficult, but wouldn't give in.

'How's your ear?' the woman asked, when he went over to join her.

O'Brien tilted his head to one side and said, dead-pan, 'Beg pardon, ma'am?'

She laughed, and looked the younger for it. 'Well,' she replied, 'I'm glad you can joke about it. That was quite a beating you took.'

He shrugged. 'It wouldn't be the first.'

'*That* I can believe. And yet — oh, nothing.'

'Go on, ma'am.'

'Well, it's just that you don't strike me as being a particularly violent man, Mr O'Brien. You don't enjoy the violence, I mean. Not like Tom Grandee or Wade Langham.'

'I never have, Mrs Farrow. But sometimes it goes with the job.'

'Then why not change jobs?'

He remembered something Joe Tucker had said to him a few days earlier. 'Because a man has to do what he does best, I guess,' he answered. 'And do it as long as he's able.'

She nodded, fell silent a moment, then announced, 'I'll be taking Dr Caulder back to examine the herd tomorrow. It shouldn't take him more than a couple of days to conduct all his tests, and if the weather turns again we can always bunk down in the line shack my husband built in the valley. It's a bit run-down, but it'll do.'

'Do you want me to come along as well?' he asked.

'You've decided to work for us after all, then?'

He showed her a crooked grin. 'I think circumstances have already decided that for me, don't you?'

'I suppose they have,' she agreed softly. 'And I suppose we should also discuss terms. The only trouble is, I can't pay you a cent until the herd is sold. We just don't have the money. But it *will* sell, I know it.'

'Don't fret about it, ma'am. I reckon you're a good enough risk.'

'I'll take that as a compliment,' she

smiled. 'As for coming with us tomorrow, I don't think there's any need. In any case, I'd prefer it if you kept an eye on things around here.'

He touched the brim of his hat and made to turn away. 'If you'll excuse me, then, I'll go get myself cleaned up.'

'Mr O'Brien?' she said.

'Yes, Mrs Farrow?'

'Thank you. Lyn and I, well . . . it's been a struggle, ever since my husband died. It's a lonely trail, you know, for a woman trying to make her way in a man's world. It has a way of . . . wearing a body down. Clay does what he can to be the man of the house, of course, but he's just a boy.'

'A *fine* boy, what I've seen of him.'

'He is, that. Anyway, I just wanted to say. It's good to have an ally, at last. Someone I feel I can trust.'

He smiled down at her. 'That's me, ma'am,' he said. 'Old dependable.'

6

That evening, Abel Spark served up a rough-and-ready supper of chicken pie, pinto beans, onions and green chillies. It wasn't the best meal O'Brien had ever eaten, but right then it was certainly the most welcome. Even Caulder, his face browned by a day under the sun, dug in with enthusiasm.

'How's Langham?' asked Jane, before the old man could leave them to it.

Spark wiped his horny palms on his shirtfront. 'Mad enough to chew tacks an' spit rust,' he replied. 'But I quietened him down with some tincture of aconite, cleaned his cuts, taped his ribs an' yanked a tooth that was more or less ready to fall out anyways. He was sleepin' like a babe, las' time I looked.'

'How soon can we be rid of him?' Lyn wanted to know.

'He'll likely be fit enough to ride on tomorrow.'

'Good. Doesn't set right with me, havin' one of Tom Grandee's men around the place. Sooner he makes dust, the better.'

After supper Jane cleared the dishes and sent her boy off to bed, and while Lyn and the others moved through the room to the more comfortable chairs set around the stone fireplace, she fixed coffee, lacing each cup with a generous measure of whiskey, which she reckoned they all deserved.

Eventually Lyn went to bed, and a short while later a yawning Caulder also said his goodnights. As he left them alone, Jane explained that she'd given the veterinarian the spare bedroom, so O'Brien would have to make do with a cot in the bunkhouse. 'I'm sorry I can't offer you something more comfortable,' she finished. 'You must be a mass of bruises.'

'Don't worry about it, ma'am. I'm

comfortable enough right where I am, at present.'

'Then stay there,' she invited, 'or use the sofa, if you prefer. You're more than welcome.'

'Bunkhouse'll do fine,' he said, rising as she prepared to follow the others to bed. 'But with your permission, I'll just sit here a while longer and finish my coffee.'

'Of course. There's more in the pot, if you've a mind.'

After she'd gone, he sank back into the rawhide chair and drained his cup. It had been a long day, and the effects of the fight, coupled with the ten-mile cattalo-drive south-west, were finally taking their toll. He closed his eyes, figuring to rest them a while, and thought about what still lay ahead for them. And gradually, without being aware of it, he too drifted off to sleep.

★   ★   ★

It was a sound that shouldn't have been there that woke him up again: something muffled by distance, dropping or falling with a clatter.

He sat up fast and glanced quickly around the room. By the flickering glow of the lantern Jane had left burning, he checked the face of the Connecticut shelf clock on the mantel and saw with mild surprise that it was a little after four in the morning.

He'd fallen asleep, then, and slept for the better part of six hours.

Feeling more than knowing that something was wrong, he came up out of the chair, crossed to the lantern and blew it out. A moment later he ghosted back across the darkened room, drew his Colt and carefully opened the door.

Outside, the sky was already starting to lighten imperceptibly, and the barn, bunkhouse, corrals and cookshack all showed as black silhouettes against the midnight blue of the firmament beyond.

He came through the door and

sidestepped to the left, listening to the night. Everything was quiet again now, save for the slow, laddery turn of the windmill behind the house and the low rustle of the cool wind as it chased itself through the long grass.

Then, just as he was about to step out of the shadows and head for the bunkhouse to check on Langham, he heard a soft, short-lived creak on the other side of the yard, and froze.

The barn door was slowly being shoved open.

Moments later a tall, powerfully built man holding a thin-looking saddle-gun in his right hand led a dark horse out into the yard. Moving carefully, as though he were favouring himself, he gathered his reins, then set about toeing in and mounting up.

It was Langham.

O'Brien barked, '*Hold it!*'

For a man who'd been doped up with aconite, however, Langham was quick to react. Already in the saddle, he twisted at the waist, brought the saddle-gun around one-handed and triggered a shot toward the sound of O'Brien's voice.

O'Brien dropped low as the heavy bullet whacked into the doorframe behind him, but even as he made to shoot back, Langham tossed the saddle-gun aside and kicked the horse — his charcoal, O'Brien now realized — to a gallop. Seconds later he vanished into the darkness, the rolling drum of his horse's hoofs following after him until even that faded to nothing.

Leathering his Colt and pushing upright again, O'Brien frowned into the dying night, not really thinking about Langham now, but thinking about the saddle-gun the other man had fired at him. Langham hadn't been carrying any such weapon earlier, so where had it come from?

Not much liking the answer, he crossed the moon-washed yard at a trot and bent to retrieve the item in question. It was a strong but spindly-looking thing: he recognized it immediately as Abel

Spark's old Burnside carbine.

And that wasn't all.

As he turned the weapon in his hands, his right palm touched something sticky on the brass butt-plate. Something that showed black in the moonlight. Something he knew was blood.

'Mr O'Brien?' It was Jane, calling from the house.

'It's all right,' he called back. 'It was Langham. He's gone.'

But what had he left behind him?

As Jane, Lyn, Caulder and Clay ventured out onto the veranda, he ran to the bunkhouse. The door there was ajar, the long room beyond in darkness.

He went inside, looked around as best he could. A cheap wooden cabinet had been overturned just inside the doorway. As he propped the carbine against the wall and bent to set it upright again, he wondered if that's what he'd heard crashing to the floor.

It was then that he heard a new sound a short distance to his left — a groan.

He turned just as the others reached the doorway and said, voice tight, 'Find a lamp. Let's get some light in here.'

'What is it?' asked Jane. 'What's happened?'

But Lyn had already worked it out. 'Where's Abel?' she asked urgently.

'Mister?' said Clay, tugging at Caulder's arm and gesturing to a socket lamp on the opposite wall. Caulder hurried over to it, located some lucifers on the shelf nearby and lit it, filling the room with a smoky yellow glow.

Jane breathed, '*Abel!*'

The old man lay sprawled on his back, just the other side of the cabinet. His thin hands were fluttering weakly on his narrow chest, and he looked as white as chalk, his eyes restless, glazed, filled with sadness and uncertainty.

Half of his head had been stove in, and he was lying in a pool of his own dark, thin blood.

Before O'Brien could move, Lyn gave a sob and shoved past him. She, like

Jane, was wearing a long, stiff nightgown, and it rustled as she threw herself down beside the old man and gently brushed his sparse white hair back off his forehead.

'M-Missy Lyn?' Spark murmured in a weak voice.

'I'm here, Abel. We're all here.'

The old man screwed his eyes shut for a moment, tried to shake his head. 'H-heard a sh-shot,' he husked. 'Langham — '

'Forget Langham,' she cut in. 'You're all that matters now.'

O'Brien knelt beside them. 'What happened, Abel?' he asked softly.

The old man looked up without really seeing him, his unfocused eyes bloodshot and racked with pain. 'H-he must've . . . come round, figured he felt a . . . sight better'n he had, an' . . . decided to make s-some more . . . trouble, I . . . guess,' he breathed. 'I was asleep . . . over yonder. Thought I'd stay close, see, so's I c'd . . . keep an eye on him. First I heard was a board, creakin' under his weight. I sat up, saw him . . . helpin' himself to my c-car-bine . . . '

'Easy, Abel,' whispered Lyn.

But the old man wanted to get it all said. 'I come up offen . . . my bunk, braced him . . . tried to take my gun back, but he . . . he punched me an' I . . . I f-fell . . . ' He swallowed noisily. 'S-sonofabuck di'n't give me no . . . chance . . . to get back up. C-came at me with . . . the carbine, used it like a club, hit me an' . . . went *on* hittin' me, jus' wouldn't *stop* . . . '

A coughing fit seized him momen-tarily, after which he continued, 'I . . . guess he got . . . tired, after a time . . . or jus' p-plain figured me fer dead. Either way, he lit out when he was . . . through with me. I t-tried to haul myself up usin' yonder . . . cabinet, but it wouldn't . . . take my weight . . . went over instead . . . '

He didn't want to give in to the pain but he couldn't help it. All at once he made a low wailing sound, and tears

shone bright in his eyes. 'Aw, Missy Lyn
..' he breathed. 'I'm hurtin' so bad . . . '

'Easy, Abel,' Lyn said again, gathering him into her lap, holding him close
and rocking him gently. 'We'll fetch
help.'

'Too late fer that . . . ' he moaned,
and started weeping softly, because he
knew he was going to leave them soon
and he didn't want to go. 'Jus' promise
me you'll all . . . look after y'selves . . . '

'You know we will, Abel,' Lyn
choked, as Spark's ruined head turned
very gently to one side. 'Abel . . . ?' she
said again.

Jaw muscles working, O'Brien reached
out and took her right arm. 'He's gone,
Lyn,' he said quietly.

For a moment she just stared at him.
Then, with the smallest shake of her
head, she mouthed the word *No*.

He nodded very deliberately, so there
would be no doubt, and told her, 'I'm
sorry,' even though there were no words
to adequately convey just how sorry he
really was.

He stood up, feeling somehow hollowed-out, and looked over at Jane. Was she thinking the same thing *he* was thinking? That if he hadn't allowed himself to fall asleep in the house, if he'd done the job Abel Spark was *killed* doing, watching Langham — ?

But Jane, like Clay and Caulder, was simply staring down at what was left of the old cook and trying to come to terms with what had just happened and why. Jane's lips were twitching, but so far she was holding her tears in check, unlike Clay, whose small shoulders were rising and falling to the rhythm of his silent sobs.

O'Brien asked in little more than a whisper, 'How do I reach Circle G from here?'

Jane blinked at him. 'No,' she replied. 'Whatever you've got in mind, forget it. There's been enough killing — '

'*Tell me*! he snapped.

'They'll be waitin' for you,' said Lyn, standing up anD turning towards him. The old man's blood had stained the front of her nightgown, and in the gloom it looked like dark, spilled ink. 'Langham, Grandee, the whole double-damned bunch of 'em.'

'Not if I can catch Langham before he reaches Circle G.'

'You'll never do that,' she replied. 'He's had too much of a head-start.'

'Then I'd better not waste any more time arguing about it,' he countered. Then he headed for the barn, a quiet, dangerous and wholly uncharacteristic anger smouldering darkly inside him.

★　★　★

Circle G, when he reached it a little after sun-up, looked much like every other cattle ranch he'd ever seen. There was a sizeable main house, a low, weathered bunkhouse split in two by a covered dog-trot, three barns, a scattering of storage sheds, two corrals, at the centre of which were set sturdy, well-worn snubbing posts, and a towering windmill built over an artesian well, its metal blades turning slowly, so that each one reflected the flame-coloured sunrise in a series of brief, blinding flares.

And there, in the starve-out close to the house, stood Langham's lathered charcoal.

Sitting his mount on a high, timbered ridge over-looking the ranch, O'Brien pursed his lips. He hadn't wanted it to come to this, a showdown on Grandee's home turf. It would've suited him better to have caught up with Langham out on the trail. But Lyn had been right — he'd had too much of a head-start for that. So here he was, about to beard the lion in his den, whether he wanted to or not.

A few horses were being exercised in the corrals. About five or six hired men were sitting on a bench just inside in the shaded dogtrot, drinking coffee, smoking cigarettes and conversing. Another man was carrying out some repairs to a wagon drawn up beside the nearest barn, and not too far from him, one more was using a long-handled axe to chop firewood.

Just another day on just another ranch, he thought — except that every man-jack down there was wearing a pistol, tied low.

Which meant they were expecting him.

Deciding not to keep them waiting any longer, he slid his Winchester from its scabbard, jacked a shell into the breech, then rode down onto the rutted trail that led into the yard, the weapon held loosely across his lap, his finger curled around the trigger.

Hearing the sound of his approach, the man repairing the wagon and his companion chopping firewood both turned his way. He wondered whether or not they'd try to brace him, but they didn't. Maybe they were under orders not to. As soon as he had passed them, however, they set down their tools and walked back up the trail behind him, effectively cutting off his retreat.

One of the men taking his ease in the

dog-trot suddenly stood up, shaded his eyes with his left hand, watched a moment, then crossed the yard at a sprint. Short and thin, with a dark skin that hinted at Spanish ancestry, he headed directly for the house and vanished inside, while his companions slowly pushed to their feet and came out into the blinding light.

O'Brien was well into the yard by this time, had slowed the blood-bay to a cautious walk and was eyeing the house, where he knew he'd find his quarry. It was a large, two-storey affair, with a wide veranda that was shaded by a tiled overhang, its timbers painted white, its small window-frames and wide front door painted green. Everything about it looked fresh and new, and it was, because the original structure had burned down in a fire that might or might not have been started by Tom Grandee: the same fire that had claimed the life of Jim Glass, who had stood between Tom and his dream of becoming a man of means.

As he reined in out front, the door swung open and out into the red, early-morning light they came — Tom Grandee, Wade Langham, the reluctant Lew Glass and the man who had alerted them all to his arrival. O'Brien saw now that his guess had been correct: this man was indeed Mexican. He was dressed in a denim jacket and Levis, and his black, curl-brimmed J.B. threw its shadow down across a narrow face that was home to dark, glittering eyes and an over-large nose. He was around thirty or so, with a pocked, copper-coloured skin and a sober mouth that was all but hidden by a thick black moustache.

Then he noticed that Tom was wearing a black band around his left arm, and he thought, *He's had the news about Al, then*. Neither was it lost on him that Langham, who'd left Jane's place unarmed, was now packing iron again: a .44 Colt Wells Fargo, sitting in the right pocket of his crossed gunbelts.

Grandee squinted up at him, a hard,

cold expression on his long, bloodless face, and in that slow, deliberate rasp of his he said, 'I di'n't hardly believe it when Javier came in with the news. But here you are, large as life.' He spat. 'You got a nerve, showing yourself around here after what you did yest'day, bushwhackin' Wade an' whuppin' the tar outa him fer no good reason.'

'Is that how Wade told it?'

'You callin' him a liar?'

'I'm just wondering if he told you he beat Abel Spark to death, as well?'

Langham grinned through still-swollen lips. 'You got no proof o' that.'

'The old man told us what happened, Wade. He lived long enough to do that.'

Langham hesitated momentarily, until the old urge to prove himself came rushing back to the surface. 'Well,' he said, seizing the chance to show off in front of his boss, 'that old belly-cheater wasn't no loss. 'Sides, we're mournin' our own dead right now.'

'Oh?' asked O'Brien, all innocence.

Tom nodded, his green cat's-eyes looking even bleaker than usual. 'My brother was killed a few days ago. Shot dead by a fatherless son of a whore who di'n't give him no chance to defend hisself. But I don't suppose you'd know anythin' about that?'

Tightening his grip on the Winchester, O'Brien replied, 'I'd know *all* about it, Tom. It was me that killed him.'

He knew he wasn't telling the one-armed man anything he didn't already know, or at least had guessed. Sharp as a tack, Tom had likely put two and two together the minute he'd heard the news.

'Then you really *have* got a nerve,' Tom remarked, stepping down into the dirt, his left hand beginning to flex in anticipation of the killing to come. 'Best you get down off that horse, O'Brien. Me an' you got business, I reckon.'

'That can wait,' O'Brien told him, trying to watch Tom, Langham and the Mexican, Javier, all at the same time — and Lew Glass, too, if it came to that. Whose side would he take when the bullets started flying?

He threw the short, overweight cattleman a quick glance in order to find out. Under his scrutiny, Glass reached up to scratch self-consciously at his oiled, fair-to-red hair. He was dressed in a collarless white shirt and an unbuttoned corduroy waistcoat, and his sleeves were rolled back to reveal fat, weak forearms. He looked tense and sweaty, just the way he'd looked during their first encounter, at The Horn A'Plenty. But he didn't glance away when O'Brien's eyes found his. Instead he stared right back with a sudden, surprising intensity, and it was a moment before O'Brien realized that what he was actually seeing in the man's feverish blue-green gaze was a desperate, fretful plea for help.

Well, that figured.

Following the death of his brother, Glass had ended up in the company of other, tougher men whose way of life and inclination towards violence scared the hell out of him. He'd doubtless learned to hate that fear and the men who inspired it, just as he'd come to despise not knowing how long he had before Tom Grandee finally decided that he, like his brother Jim before him, had outlived his usefulness.

All of which told O'Brien that he might well have an ally here, if he was lucky.

'I ain't waitin', O'Brien,' growled Tom, his hand starting to flex faster, more urgently.

'You're gonna have to, Tom,' said O'Brien. 'I've got business with your friend here, first.'

'An' what business would that be?' demanded Langham.

'I'm exercising my right to make a citizen's arrest,' said O'Brien.

Langham looked incredulous. 'You *what*?'

'You heard me. You murdered Abel Spark, Langham, and if I've got anything to do with it, you'll hang for the deed.'

A low chuckle issued from between Langham's twisted lips, but it was a quick, nervous sound that tried hard to come out tough and indifferent, and failed on both counts. 'You think I'll stand for that?' he asked.

Bringing the Winchester up so that the stock was resting on his hip, the barrel pointing skyward, O'Brien said, 'Nope. I think you'll reach for that gun on your hip — and I'll save the hangman a chore.'

Something in Langham's eyes went very flat and very dangerous. He tilted his head first one way, then the other, and as the bones there gave an audible crack, he said, 'You're crazy.'

A split second later he went for his gun.

*　*　*

O'Brien knew what was coming long before Langham finally made his move.

He'd seen it in the way Langham's legs and shoulders had suddenly tensed up, the way his fingers had stiffened ever so slightly and made the bones in the back of his gun-hand stand proud. He'd seen it in the gritting of Langham's teeth and the quickening of his breathing, and because of all that he was ready for it.

So —

The second Langham's right hand closed around the grips of the .44 and started to tear it from leather, he brought the Winchester down in one swift chopping motion and squeezed the trigger, and propelled by sixty grains of black powder, his .45/.60 centre-fire cartridge blew a small, tidy hole right through Langham's throat.

Langham lurched backwards under the impact, jerked his own trigger reflexively and sent a bullet into the hardpan at his feet. Then the gun slipped from his fingers and he grabbed for his punctured windpipe, looking wide-eyed, slack-jawed, completely, utterly surprised by what had happened to him.

The blink of an eye later he keeled

over, dead before he hit the ground.

Working the lever one-handed to put a fresh shell under the hammer, O'Brien swung the Winchester's octagonal barrel around to cover Tom and Javier. 'Don't,' he hissed, as his spooked horse danced a little to one side.

Both men froze halfway through hauling iron, although the air around them remained charged with tension, the prospect of further violence — not only from Tom and Javier but from any or all of the gunmen surrounding them — still no more than a hammer-click away.

Then Javier straightened up, carefully brought his slender hands away from his sides in a gesture of compliance. Behind him, Lew Glass continued to gawp at Langham's corpse, his expression one of shock and revulsion.

Of the three, only Tom still wanted to make trouble. His eyes kept shuttling from O'Brien's face to the business end of his Winchester and back again, figuring the odds. 'Forget it, Tom,'

O'Brien cautioned, his voice flat and authoritative. 'You'll get another chance before this is all over.'

But Tom, unpredictable, hair-trigger Tom, was already beginning to tremble as the need to kill threatened to consume him, and the fingers of his left hand started flexing again, fast, faster, until they were almost a blur. 'You ain't leavin' here breathin', O'Brien,' he grated. 'Not after what you did to my brother.' His on-off smile suddenly came and went. ''Any case, we got you whipsawed, you sonofabitch. You ain't goin' *nowhere*.'

O'Brien had a sneaking suspicion that Tom was right about that. He was surrounded by the friends of his enemy, and even if Tom had given specific orders to leave him be, that he was Tom's alone for the killing, there was nothing to stop any one of them from trying to bring him down with a shot that would only wound. Then he really *would* find himself at Tom's questionable mercy.

Tom himself was evidently thinking along the same lines. 'Ah, man,' he rasped, 'I'm gonna enjoy watchin' you squirm before you die.'

His fingers continued flexing, flexing, flexing, and any moment now he was going to slap leather and then all hell would break loose.

Until —

'Don't do it, Grandee! You're a dead man if you do!'

The yelled warning sliced through the tension of the moment, the voice tight, hard, determined. Jarred by it, Tom's eyes flickered to the right, to someplace beyond O'Brien and, as he heard a low, ominous mutter rumble through the men surrounding them, O'Brien chanced a brief look that way himself, just to make sure his ears weren't deceiving him.

They weren't.

Lyn Merrick, dressed now in hurriedly donned pants, shirt and jacket, was sitting her paint horse beside the half-repaired wagon about forty yards away, the reins dallied around her saddle horn and a Henry repeater in her fists, the stock pressed against her right cheek, the barrel lined up on Tom's narrow chest.

'Hear me?' she called. 'You or any other man here makes a move agin O'Brien, you take a bullet, Tom. 'Fact, I might jus' let you have a bullet anyway, mood I'm in right now!'

Seeing Lyn, hearing her, guessing that she had come after him because there'd be no way a woman of her character could ever have done otherwise, O'Brien felt a sudden rush of admiration coupled with no small measure of relief. But Tom, as he recovered himself, only showed his broken, yellow teeth in a sneer. 'You ain't got the stomach for it, lady,' he replied easily.

'Try me,' she invited.

He glared at her for a long moment, clearly evaluating her, and she found it hard not to look away. Then, at last, he nodded. 'All right,' he said, and puffing his chest out, he slapped it hard, dead centre, with his left hand. 'Go on, then. Right here oughta do it!'

It was the last thing she'd been expecting, this invitation to kill, and when she hesitated, still shaken by having witnessed Langham's violent death, Tom took a pace forward, spurs jangling discordantly, balled his fist and again hit himself hard in the chest. 'Well, what you waitin' for, you ornery bitch?' he demanded. 'Pull the goddam trigger, put me down . . . if you got the guts for it.'

'Oh, I got the guts,' Lyn called back in a low, breathless voice.

But still she held back.

Emboldened by her seeming reluctance, Tom took another spur-tinkling step forward, another, punched himself in the chest again, and now his fury was such that he could barely contain it. 'Then why don't you prove it, huh?' he roared.

'I wouldn't push her too far, was I you,' O'Brien murmured, trying to dent

Tom's growing confidence, and spare Lyn the agony of having to take a life, even one as worthless as Tom's. 'She lost a good friend today, and she's hurting.'

But that only made Tom laugh. 'She'll be hurtin' a damn'-sight worse when I'm through with her!' he snarled, and hit himself again. 'Come on, you bitch, right here! Do it, or get your nose the hell outa my business!'

Lyn drew a shuddery breath. 'Well,' she called back, 'that's plain enough, I guess.'

And sitting a little straighter in the saddle, turning her right arm just a notch in order to steady the repeater . . . she pulled the trigger.

7

Her slug struck a spot barely two inches to the right of Tom's boots and sent dirt geysering up across the toes. Instinctively he leapt to the left and reared back a pace, but almost immediately she worked the lever and fired again, and again her bullet hit the ground just ahead of him, the slug spraying dirt up over his whipcord britches and forcing him to take another backward step that brought off-key music from his spur-hung heels.

His growled oath was drowned by her third shot, which again ploughed into the earth just to Tom's right, forcing him to take another sidestep to the left, and then she worked the lever once more and fired a fourth bullet which spattered his legs with chunks of hardpan and made him retreat still further.

Tom stood his ground after that, damned if he'd move again, and was just about to call her bluff once and for all when he suddenly became aware of a nearby buzzing and realized just what she'd done.

She'd deliberately herded him towards a spot right beside Langham's corpse, so that he couldn't help but smell the metallic stink of spilled blood and hear the flies as they settled on the body and started wandering in and out of the folds of the dead man's shirt, looking for something to feed on.

Drawing a bead on his chest, Lyn asked, 'You really sure you want to join Langham in hell, Tom?'

He looked at her again, seeing her in a new light, and O'Brien reckoned he could pretty well read Tom's mind now. She could shoot, he was thinking, and she'd made her point as neat as could be. But could she kill him? He didn't look quite so doubtful anymore. And in his expression something else began to show itself — the realization that, if she *did* kill him, he'd never get the chance to settle things for brother Al.

Discretion, then, was the better part of valour.

'All right, lady!' he yelled at last, clearly hating himself for it. 'All right, so you're feelin' real mean this mornin'. Well, OK. You got us all quakin'.' He turned his green cat's-eyes on O'Brien and waved dismissively. 'Make dust,' he snarled. 'Go on, *get*. Al an' me, we can wait, I reckon.'

Keeping his face neutral, O'Brien slowly backed the blood-bay away from the house, keeping his eye on Tom, on Javier, on as many of them as it was possible to watch all at once, and he was relying on Lyn to watch the men he couldn't see from this angle, the men who might even yet try to take the two of them together, and turn Tom's defeat into a dreadful victory.

At last the yard receded and he drew level with Lyn. 'All right,' he said, keeping his eyes on the men standing like cigar-store Indians all around the yard, 'I got you covered. Now get the heck out of here. I'll be right behind you.'

She shoved the Henry into its sheath and unwound her reins. 'I'll wait for you at the top of yonder rise.'

Then she turned her mount and, at a gallop headed for the ridge from which O'Brien had first surveyed the ranch. When she topped out a couple of minutes later, he spun his own mount around and whacked the rifle barrel against its rump to get it moving.

'*Yaah*!'

The horse gave him every ounce of speed it could muster, and gave still more when an angry scattering of shots firecrackered after them. Then Tom started yelling and the gunfire petered out, leaving man and beast free to ascend the slope without having to dodge more lead.

When he finally joined her on level ground, he and Lyn looked back at the men below as they gathered around Langham's body. 'You reckon they'll come after us?' asked the girl.

'I doubt it. Tom'll try *something*, that's for sure, but it won't be any time soon.' He glanced at her, said, 'That was pretty good shooting, by the way.'

'I didn't kill him, though, did I?' she countered, clearly disgusted with herself. 'When it came to it, I didn't have the guts.'

'Believe me, Lyn, it wouldn't have made you feel any better if you had.'

'It made you feel better to kill Langham, though.'

His face clouded. 'Not so's you'd notice. Anyway, you did fine enough as it was. That took nerve, and I'm beholden.'

To his surprise, she found within her a crooked smile. 'We're long on nerve around here, O'Brien, so you're in good company. Now, what say we ride?'

They rode.

★　★　★

By the time they got back to Long Branch, Jane had washed Abel Spark down, combed his flyaway hair flat and dressed him in his best go-to-meeting suit, so he was about as ready for burying as he was ever likely to get. According to Lyn, she, Jane and Clay were the closest thing the old cook had ever had to family, and for that reason Caulder had offered to dig a fresh grave in the Farrow family plot, a small, neatly tended area enclosed by a white picket fence, a few hundred yards north of the ranch.

While O'Brien turned their horses out in the corral, Lyn offered the others a brief account of what had happened at Circle G. When she was finished, Jane — who'd already agreed with Caulder to postpone their return to the high country for a day or so — said, 'I didn't think things were going to take this turn. I thought there might be *trouble*, yes, but not . . . '

Breaking off, she looked directly at the young veterinarian, whose sweated face was smeared with the odd streak of dirt. 'What I'm trying to say is, things are likely to get worse before they get better, Doctor, and this isn't your fight. If you, ah, decided to leave now, none of us would hold it against you.'

Caulder touched the healing cut on his still-bruised cheek. 'I appreciate that, Mrs Farrow. But you engaged me to do a job. I believe I'll see it through.'

Later that afternoon they laid the old man to rest, and though he listened in silence while Jane read from the Bible and Lyn said a few personal words about her beloved Abel, O'Brien's eyes constantly strayed back to the ranch and the rise and fall of the land beyond it, wondering when Tom and his men would come and what they would do when they got here.

Then the service, such as it was, was over, and a tearful Clay broke away from the rest of them and went racing back toward the house, head down, fists clenched.

Darkness fell, and they ate a modest supper without noticeable appetite, after which O'Brien excused himself and went over to the bunkhouse, which Lyn had cleaned up earlier in the day. He set an old ladderback chair just inside the open doorway and sat with his rifle on his lap, waiting. The night was quiet, and a cool wind was blowing from the south-east. If Tom Grandee's men came from that direction, he'd hear them long before they arrived.

But Tom's men didn't come.

The night passed quietly and a little after first light he awoke from a shallow doze feeling gritty-eyed and stiff of back. He pumped water, shaved, then crossed to the house, where he found Jane in the kitchen, her back to him as she filled a gunnysack with supplies in preparation for her trip back into the hills.

'You look busy,' he observed by way of greeting.

Taken by surprise, she threw him a brief, over-the-shoulder glance, then continued packing. Without turning around again, she cleared her throat and said, 'Bad night. Figured I'd be better up and doing.'

She was hoping to sound casual and in control, but her voice, sounding husky and nasal instead, told a different story. She'd been crying, and without meaning to, he'd blundered in and caught her at it.

Realizing as much, he murmured, 'I'll, ah, be checking on my horse, if you need me,' and made to withdraw.

Before he could leave, however, Jane stopped what she was doing and said softly, 'It seems so quiet without Abel stamping around.'

He hesitated, allowed, 'He was a caution, right enough.'

'And he didn't deserve to die the way he did,' she muttered bitterly.

'No, ma'am, he didn't.'

There was a long, uncomfortable pause, during which she continued to look down into the sack she'd been filling, and it was a moment before he realized she was crying again.

'Easy, Mrs Farrow,' he said. He would have preferred to say something less dumb, but he didn't really know what. 'Easy, now. You're not finished yet.'

Hearing that, she spun, looked him right in the face with tears like molten silver sliding down her cheeks, and once again he saw a woman beaten down by life and on the verge of giving up the fight altogether.

Then, before he could do, say or think anything more, she came forward in a rush and buried her face in his shoulder, and all the pain, hurt, doubt and fear she'd kept bottled up for so long suddenly came out in a dam-burst of sobs.

'Easy, ma'am,' he said again, awkwardly. He knew she needed to be held, that it had been too long since she'd felt a man's arms around her, offering protection and solace, but he hesitated to accommodate her in case she took his actions the wrong way. When she continued to weep without let-up, however, he thought, *The hell with it*, and reached out to pull her close.

'Let it go, Mrs Farrow,' he said in a whisper. 'Let it all go.'

She did. And God help him, as he felt her silky, fragrant, copper-coloured hair brushing gently against the line of his jaw, he became keenly, uncomfortably aware of her warmth, her *smell*, the *softness* of her and the undeniable fact that she was indeed a *woman*.

'You . . . you say we're n-not finished yet,' she stammered a short time later, her voice muffled by his shirt, 'b-but it . . . it's only a matter of time, isn't it? We don't really stand a prayer against Grandee, do we?'

He pushed her away from him gently, held her firmly by the elbows and was just about to reply when he suddenly turned toward the window instead, and snapped, 'Rider coming.'

Dabbing at her eyes with her apron, Jane squinted through the glass just as a single horseman skylined himself on the eastern ridge, then put his horse down the near slope, headed for the ranch.

'It's Dale Weavers,' she reported,

sounding vaguely surprised. Catching the question in O'Brien's glance, she explained, 'He's the marshal's deputy, or leastways he *was*. I heard tell he lost his job when the hoof-and-mouth more or less turned Elkhorn into a ghost town, but maybe I was mistaken.'

'Well, he's wearing a badge *now*,' O'Brien pointed out. 'And that means we'd better go see what he wants, I guess.'

They went outside just as the newcomer trotted his chunky dun into the yard and drew rein. 'Morning, Dale,' Jane greeted cautiously. 'Help you?'

Weavers was a tall, undernourished man about thirty years old, whose spare, sallow face was dominated by dark, unblinking eyes and a thin, unsmiling mouth. Beneath his calfskin vest he wore a striped cotton shirt tucked into grey cords, the cords stuffed into high, square-toed boots.

'Mrs Farrow,' he replied. He had a lightly pocked skin and fine, collar-length black hair that stuck out beneath his grey felt hat, and he wore his gun — a single-action Colt .45 — high around his narrow waist. 'Like to have a word with your, uh, hired man here, if I may.'

'Oh?'

'Yes'm. They's been a complaint, I'm afeared. Serious.'

'I guess you'd better step down and come inside, then.'

Weavers cooled his three-quarter rig, tied his horse to one of the porch uprights and followed them back inside, where Lyn, Caulder and Clay, still looking puffy-eyed from sleep, had been roused by the lawman's arrival.

Weavers offered them a short, businesslike nod, then turned to O'Brien and said, 'Understand you killed Tom Grandee's foreman yest'day.'

O'Brien made no attempt to deny it. 'It was a fair fight. He drew first.'

'That's not the way I heard it,' the deputy replied grimly. 'Accordin' to Tom Grandee, you'd been pushing Wade Langham for quite a spell before you killed him. Beat him with your fists, abducted him, then shot him dead when he got away from you. That makes it sound more like murder to me.'

'That's a lie!' Lyn cut in hotly. 'Wade killed Abel Spark!'

'You got witnesses to that?'

'We heard the truth of it from Abel's own lips before he died,' retorted Lyn.

'But you got no one who actually *saw* it happen?'

'Abel wasn't given to telling lies, Dale,' Jane said stiffly. 'And certainly not as he lay dying.'

The deputy raised one hand. 'No call to get het up, Mrs Farrow. I know Abel was close to you-all. But Tom Grand-ee's sworn out a complaint against this man here, an' he's got all the witnesses a body could wish for — which makes it a matter for the court. That bein' the case, O'Brien, I'm gonna have to ask you to surrender your gun an' accompany me back to town.'

Lyn asked in disbelief, 'Are you

arrestin' him, Dale?'

'Yes, Miss Merrick, I am. An' not without good reason. Seems O'Brien here also left two dead men behind him in Skeeter Creek — one of 'em Mr Grandee's brother.'

O'Brien's teeth set hard. Of all the things he'd thought Tom might do, involving the law hadn't been one of them. It made sense, though, because if Weavers took him in, there'd be no one here to stop Tom from finally making his move against Long Branch. Jane, Lyn, Caulder, Clay, the herd — they'd be easy pickings, the lot of them.

'I got a better idea,' he said. 'Suppose I stop by your office later today and give you and your boss *my* side of the story? I'll make a statement, sign it and swear to it before the pair of you. Then, if you've got any other questions, I'll answer 'em at the inquest.'

'An' in the meantime,' Weavers said mockingly, 'we turn you loose an' hope you don't light out first chance you get, is that it?'

'No,' Jane countered hurriedly. 'You put him in my custody.'

Weavers' eyebrows rose in surprise. 'Say *what*, ma'am?'

'I'd trust Mr O'Brien with my life, Dale. And even if he *was* guilty — which, by the way, he isn't — I know he'd never run off and leave me to face the consequences.'

Lyn nodded agreement. 'That's reasonable, isn't it, Dale?'

Weavers pulled a face. 'I'm sorry, ma'am, but I don't think it is. 'Case it's slipped your mind, three men have already died by this man's hand.'

'But there's a difference between *killing* a man and *murdering* him,' Jane argued.

'Mrs Farrow's right,' said Caulder. 'The only reason Mr O'Brien killed Tom Grandee's brother and this other man, Weedon, was to stop them from killing me. Check with Sheriff Tucker at Skeeter Creek, if you won't take my word for it. He was satisfied that Mr O'Brien acted in defence of my life and his own.'

'An' don't forget *me*, Dale,' added Lyn. 'I saw what happened at Circle G yest'day mornin'. O'Brien was all for makin' a citizen's arrest, but Wade went for his gun — an' I'd be more'n happy to swear to it.'

Weavers studied them for a long moment, drawing air through his beak of a nose before finally saying, 'You folks sure talk up a good argument. But it's not my decision to make. Still . . . we'll do like you say, O'Brien. You come on back to town with me an' speak your piece to the marshal himself. We'll let him decide what's to be done with you.'

Lyn said quietly, 'You'll get a fair shake from Marshal Cobb, O'Brien. He's a good man, an' he's no friend of Tom's.'

O'Brien nodded, not much wanting to go but knowing this was about as much of a concession as he was likely to get in the circumstances. Turning to Weavers, he said, 'I'll go fetch my horse.'

By the time he'd saddled up and led the blood-bay out into the building sunshine, Weavers had already remounted the dun, and Jane and the others had gathered soberly on the veranda to see him off.

'I'll be back soon as I can, ma'am,' he said, lifting to the saddle.

'We'll be watching for you,' Jane replied softly.

He and Weavers put their horses to the far ridge, climbed at a canter in silence, then started down the blind side — and straight into the path of eight horsemen who were blocking the unmarked trail forty yards ahead of them.

They'd been invisible from the ranch, of course, hidden by the high swell of land that also masked the series of tall-grass hills beyond, but there was no missing them now, just as there was no mistaking who they were: as he recognized Tom, Javier and the half-dozen other men he'd seen at Circle G the day before, O'Brien immediately drew in and reached for his .38.

'*Don't!*' barked Weavers, shortening rein a few feet behind him.

Hipping around, O'Brien saw that the deputy had already drawn and thumb-cocked his own Colt and had it aimed at the small of his back, and when he saw that he realized, too late, that he'd been set up.

Jane, he remembered, had said she'd thought Weavers had lost his job. It looked like she'd been right. But somehow he'd held onto his badge instead of handing it in, and found himself a new employer — Tom.

And the object of the deception?

Simply to get him away from Long Branch.

At the ranch, he would've had cover. Out here, he had nothing. At a pinch, he could have organized Jane and the others into a rough-and-ready fighting force to repel any attack. But isolate him, lure him out into the open, put him beside a man he'd thought he could trust, a man who'd just as soon stick a gun in his ribs, and he was at Tom's mercy.

A sudden flare of anger coursed through him, anger that he could have fallen so easily for Weavers' fine talk of murder charges and arrests. And he felt a fair degree of apprehension as well, because he knew this was going to end badly for him, perhaps the worst way possible.

He turned back towards Tom just as the one-armed man, his narrow torso once again hidden beneath the folds of his All-Around duster, kicked his sorrel to speed and started closing the distance between them at a hard run. The men with him, Lew Glass conspicuous by his absence, bunched up behind him, each one carrying his pistol in hand.

Again O'Brien glanced at Weavers, looking for an opening, any chance at all. But there wasn't one, leastways none that he could see. In any case, Tom and the others were almost upon them now, fanning out to surround him, and Tom himself was drawing up alongside, turning his reins around his saddle horn before reaching crosswise for his .44, his belligerent eyes alive with anticipation, his thin lips peeled back over ragged teeth.

To his left, Weavers said eagerly, 'Said I could snare him for you, didn't I?'

Tom nodded, weighing the gun slowly in his hand, not once taking his unholy gaze from O'Brien's face. 'Yeah. You snared him good, Dale.'

'So the deal stands?' Weavers prodded anxiously.

'Deal stands,' growled Tom. 'Come next election, I'm backin' you for marshal. One way or another, you' gonna win that election, Dale, an' between us we're gonna send Cobb packin'. My word on it.'

Weavers, sounding relieved now, set the hammer down on his Colt, stuffed it away and gathered up his reins. 'I'll be, ah, gettin' along, then.'

'Stick around,' murmured Tom, continuing to stare at O'Brien. 'You ain't finished here, yet.'

With an uneasy nod, Weavers hurried his dun through the knot of gunnies surrounding them, then turned the animal around so that he could watch whatever happened next from a safe distance. Another man — Javier, O'Brien thought — immediately moved in to fill the void to his left.

'Well, well,' mused Tom.

He moved then, like lightning. He brought his pistol up and around, figuring to smash O'Brien's teeth down his throat, but O'Brien, knowing he had nothing to lose, reached out, grabbed Tom's gun-hand by the wrist and rough-yanked him forward and down.

With a yelp Tom came out of the saddle, crashed to the ground between the horses and started cursing. But O'Brien's moment of triumph was short-lived. Javier crowded him from behind, cracked him across the head with the butt of his gun, and though his hat absorbed some of the blow, it still packed enough of a punch to make lights explode behind his eyes.

Before he could recover, Tom leapt back to his feet, leathered his Colt and hauled him off his horse. O'Brien slammed against the ground, trying to fight off the effects of the pistol-whipping, but even as he made to regain his feet, Tom's shadow spilled across him and Tom himself booted him hard in the side.

The impact against his already-punished ribs was excruciating, and he tried to roll away but came up against his horse's legs. The horse immediately side-hopped away from him, but the momentary delay gave Tom all the time he needed to close in and kick him again, this time driving the air from his lungs. Disorientated, O'Brien made a grab for his tormentor's ankle, missed, and Tom stamped down on his left hand, breaking something, maybe a finger.

The one-armed man really went to work on him then, while the men around them yelled and whistled their encouragement. And as the kicks came harder and faster, each one accompanied by the jarring, off-key ring of Tom's spurs, O'Brien's world was reduced to one of pain, noise and chaos.

At length, sweating hard and gasping for air, Tom backed off, grabbed for his canteen and drank. A tiny voice inside O'Brien's jumbled mind told him, *It's over.* But then, having refreshed himself, Tom reached down, rolled him onto his side and went back to work, kicking him in the belly. After the third or fourth kick, O'Brien heard — and felt — at least one of his ribs break with a muted pop.

Eventually, some long, timeless while later, the battering *did* end.

Tom, now clearly exhausted, fell loosely to his knees and glared down at his victim through pleasure-glazed eyes. He spat in O'Brien's face and then punched him spitefully in the mouth, and O'Brien, in no condition to ward it off, experienced a sudden, blinding flare of light, and then —

★ ★ ★

Nothing.

A long, incalculable period of it. No sound, no light, no feeling.

And then, all at once, a sudden, nauseating sensation of surfacing from a dark, bottomless lake, of rising quickly — *too* quickly — towards a murky halflight, and of trading a place of peace and tranquillity for a world full of pain.

He heard himself say, 'Uhhnnn . . . '

And then, as he grew increasingly aware of his injuries, of his tightly strapped chest and the strong stink of liniment, he rolled onto his side and dryretched.

'Steady, now, Mr O'Brien,' said a faraway voice he thought he recognized.

'You're all right now . . . '

He opened his eyes — the effort drained him — and when his blurred vision cleared a little, he saw Rae Caulder leaning over him. 'Clay,' the vet said, turning away momentarily. 'Go fetch some water, will you?'

O'Brien turned his head a notch, saw Lyn standing a few feet away, Clay heading for the door behind her in a hurry.

As near as he could tell, he was stretched out on a large timber-and-rawhide bed, his head in danger of being swallowed whole by a gloriously soft pillow. Lamplight showed him a cheap wardrobe beside which stood a pair of dainty, high-sided boots, and a dressing-table with a flaking mirror. Jane's room, he decided, because the pillow still carried the same fragrance he'd noticed on her that morning. At least he *thought* it was that morning.

'How . . . long . . . ?' he scratched out in someone else's voice.

'They beat you pretty thoroughly,' Caulder told him gently. 'You've been out most of the day.'

Slowly, the pain in his face, chest, stomach and arms helping to sharpen his memory, he asked, 'How . . . bad is it?'

'You've got a couple of broken ribs an' a broken finger,' supplied Lyn. 'Ain't much of you that's not bruised, cut or swollen. But Caulder here's patched you up, best he could. Says what you need now is *rest*.'

Clay came back into the room, carrying an enamel cup carefully by the base and handle. Caulder helped O'Brien to lift his head, then held the cup to his cracked lips so that he could drink.

He didn't think drinking water could wear a man out so fast, but his heart was racing and his forehead was pebbled with sweat by the time he was finished, and he was glad when Caulder helped settle him back on the pillow. 'What happened?' he breathed.

Lyn said, 'Grandee came.' And then, 'He took the herd.'

O'Brien's jaw clamped hard. His look told her to go on.

'A little while after you an' Dale rode out, Tom and his men came in, trailin' you belly-down across your horse,' she said, shock and anger making her voice tremble. 'We thought you was dead at first. Then Tom said you would be, if Jane didn't sign ownership of the herd over to Circle G.'

'You should've . . . called his bluff,' O'Brien croaked.

'That's easy to say,' she replied bitterly. 'You didn't have to make the choice.'

'But Jane *did*.'

'Yeah. She took one look at you, broken like you was, an' with Tom pointin' his gun at your head, an' said he could have the herd an' be damned. Tom gave her a bill of sale he'd already made out, got her to sign it an' then had Dale Weavers witness it, jus' to make it legal.'

'Did he . . . pay for the herd?'

'On paper, sure. But the deal was for your life, an' that's what we got.'

O'Brien stared up at the ceiling for a moment, trying to get his still-sluggish mind to work properly, but his stomach was cramping and he was starting to

feel slightly sick again. 'He can't
. . . move the herd till it's been declared
free of . . . disease,' he husked, thinking
aloud. 'We can still — '

'He has his declaration,' Caulder
said in a low, thick voice. 'I signed it
for him.' His hazel-green eyes,
meeting those of the man in the bed,
were suddenly large and fraught. 'God
help me, Mr O'Brien, he threatened
to kill you and the boy *both* if I
didn't.'

O'Brien asked, 'Where's Jane now?'

'They took her with em,' said Lyn,
her lower lip starting to work. 'They
needed her to take 'em to the herd, an'
I reckon they plan to keep her until
Grandee's got everythin' sewn up with
the authorities at White River. Whatever
she does or says after that won't matter
much. It'll be our word against his bill
of sale — an' we can't prove a damn'
thing.'

'Mister,' Clay said suddenly, 'is my
ma gonna be all right?'

O'Brien looked at him, thought

about what he'd already been through in his young life, and didn't really know what to say. Finally he settled on, 'She'll be home again real soon, son. I promise.' Then, to Lyn he asked, 'What happened to Weavers after he witnessed the bill of sale?'

She shrugged. 'He went back to town, I guess.'

He felt like death now and guessed he must look just as bad. But he couldn't afford the time it would take to heal, not if he was to do what he'd signed on to do and get Jane and her folks out of this mess. Clenching his teeth against the pain, he tried to sit up but didn't make a very convincing job of it. The room started slipping and sliding around him, and he felt an unpleasant grating in his chest that might have been the protest of his recently set ribs.

Lyn said, 'Don't get any ideas, O'Brien. Tom warned us against makin' trouble for him, an' as long as he's holdin' Jane, we're doin' jus' like he says. Besides, goin' after him, that's jus' what he *wants* you to do.'

'You think I don't know that?' O'Brien replied, with no option but to sink back onto the pillow. 'That's the only reason he didn't kill me earlier and have done with it. He wants to enjoy this, and there's no fun to be had in killing a man who's not awake to feel it, not for the likes of Tom. While I'm alive, he knows I'll go after him, that there'll be a reckoning. And that gives him something to look forward to.'

'But the state you're in right now, he'd chew you up and spit you out.'

'Could . . . be,' he allowed. 'But I've still got to do it.'

'Just leave it,' she begged.

He shook his head, said with a sigh, 'You don't understand, Lyn. Stealing your herd, stealing your sister, beating me half to death and threatening Clay . . . by doing all that, Tom's finally drawn down the lightning.'

His eyes suddenly bored into hers. 'And now,' he finished softly, 'he's gonna find out what it's like when lightning *strikes*.'

8

Reluctantly accepting the fact that he wasn't going anywhere any time soon, he asked Lyn for a shot of Jane's whiskey — a generous one — and that took the edge off the pain and went some of the way towards curbing his impatience.

Although he remained plagued by persistent stomach cramps and the constant throbbing of his broken finger, he gradually drifted back to sleep, and it was a little after ten o'clock the following morning when he cracked his eyes again and slowly took stock. His assorted hurts had settled to a general stiffness cut through with the occasional stabbing pain, and he knew he'd have to move carefully from now on, or risk undoing all Caulder's handiwork.

How he got dressed, then, remained a mystery to him, even after he'd done it. He managed everything but his socks and boots, then limped outside, washed and flopped down on a narrow bench outside the cookshack. A short while later, Lyn fetched him a cup of whiskey-laced coffee and some kind of mushy broth she'd fixed up, and though he didn't have much of an appetite, he forced it down because he knew the food would give him strength.

A few hours later he shuffled back into the house and asked Clay to help him drag his boots on. Though hampered by the broken finger on his left hand, he had no trouble buckling his gunbelt all by himself.

Coming on sunset, he forced down a little more of Lyn's broth, took another jolt of whiskey and shoved his head into a pan of cold water to chase away the worst of his lingering headache. Finally, he asked Lyn to saddle the blood-bay for him, and pack him some provisions.

'*Now?*' she breathed. 'You're leavin' now? It'll be full dark in less than an hour!'

'Just get me those provisions, will you?' he croaked wearily.

When he carefully stepped up to leather fifteen minutes later, Lyn murmured tearfully, 'We're not goin' to see you again, are we?'

'Sure you will,' he told her, adding gently, 'Missy Lyn.'

After that he rode steadily through the gathering darkness, headed north-east instead of south-west, and though the cool night air helped to clear his head a little more, he still had to stop once, when the world started spinning again.

The moon was rising by the time he reached Circle G. Aside from a light showing at one of the ground-floor windows of the main house, and another burning at a window on the first floor, the ranch looked more or less deserted.

He dismounted beside the first of the three barns. The wagon which had occupied the same spot two days earlier was nowhere in sight, so he left his horse ground-hitched in its place. Then, sticking to the shadows, he edged closer to the house.

He was about sixty feet away when a shadow passed across the ground-floor window. Immediately he tucked at the knees, drew the .38 and waited with held breath. A few moments later the shadow moved back the other way.

It was the shadow of Lew Glass.

He pushed up again, moved closer. At length, sweating hard, he reached the house, put his back to the wall beside the lit window and peered inside.

Beyond the lace curtain lay a decent-sized parlour furnished with two leather armchairs and a red horse-hair sofa. A lamp burning on a small table beside one of the chairs showed him an empty bookcase and a sideboard upon which sat an array of liquor bottles. Glass, the room's sole inhabitant, was slouched in one of the chairs, drinking whiskey from a tumbler.

Backing away from the window,

O'Brien ghosted along the covered porch until he reached the front door. There, he threw one final glance around the silent ranch, then reached for the handle, twisted and let himself into a darkened hallway.

About sixteen feet ahead, a broad staircase led up to the first floor. A light was burning up there, as he'd noticed from outside, but when he listened, the only sound he could hear was Glass, muttering drunkenly to himself in the parlour.

Satisfied that the rancher was alone, he light-footed across to the parlour door, grabbed the handle and shoved inside, fast.

Glass came out of his chair with a yelp, the tumbler falling from his hand to bounce on the thin carpet and puddle whiskey between his booted feet. 'No!' he choked, as the blood leached from his jowly, booze-flushed face. 'No, please. It w-wasn't me. It was all Tom's — '

'Shut up,' O'Brien snapped.

But Glass continued babbling, raising his pudgy hands as if he could deflect the bullet he felt sure was coming. 'You've got to believe me! I didn't want anythin' to do with it! I said it was madness! But there was nothin' I could do or say that would make him change his mind!'

In the low lamplight his blue-green eyes suddenly turned watery. ''Case you never noticed,' he finished petulantly, 'my word doesn't carry much weight around here. It never *did*.'

'That could change,' said O'Brien, putting the gun away.

Screwing up his face, Glass sulked, 'I'm no good with riddles.'

'I'll say it plain, then. I'm going after Tom — and I want you to come with me.'

Horrified by the prospect, Glass quickly shook his head. 'Oh, no, you can forget that. Tom's got a half-dozen gunnies to back him. All you've got is *you*.'

'I'm not asking you to *fight*.'

'Fight, talk, pray, run, what's the difference? If Tom knew I was even thinkin' about goin' against him, he'd kill me.'

'You're a dead man anyway, Lew,' O'Brien pointed out. 'As long as Circle G's worthless — which it is because of the hoof-and-mouth — Tom's happy to leave it in your hands. But if he pulls off this deal, gets enough money to put the ranch back on its feet, he'll want it all for himself and he'll do whatever it takes to make you to sign it over to him. The minute you do that, you're finished. You'll have out-lived your usefulness — just like your brother.'

Glass said stiffly, 'I think you'd better go — '

'I hope you're sure about that,' O'Brien replied, starting to feel a little light-headed again. ''Cause I'm all that stands between you and Tom, and you *know* it. Without me, you're dead for sure. But you help me nail him, you might just come out of this a better man. A man who didn't die before his time. A man other men could *respect*.'

For a moment then Glass stared at him, his befuddled mind racing. O'Brien could see that he wanted to stand up for himself, but that the fear with which he'd lived for so long had become a palpable, crippling thing.

'I — ' he said at last. 'I — '

Then his eyes went wide again, and O'Brien had a sudden, awful feeling that something he hadn't counted on was just about to happen.

'*Hold it!*' snapped a voice behind him.

His shoulders slumped and he swore with feeling. Ignoring the command, he turned and asked, 'What the hell are *you* doing here?' Then, remembering the light he'd seen burning at the upstairs window, 'Keeping an eye on Glass, is that it? Making sure he holds his nerve till this is all over?'

'Somethin' like that,' replied Dale Weavers. The former deputy was standing in the open doorway, hatless, his Colt held close to his hip and pointed O'Brien's way. 'Now, get your hands up.'

'I don't think so, Dale.'

'Get 'em up, damn you!'

'Or what?' countered O'Brien. 'What're you gonna do? Shoot me? I don't reckon Tom'd cotton much to that. He's looking forward to handling that little chore himself.'

'Best you don't push me an' find out,' Weavers snarled. He made a rough gesture with his gun that told O'Brien he should turn around or else, and this time he complied, but only so that he could look directly at Glass.

'Remember what I said, Lew,' he murmured. 'I'm all that stands between you and Tom.'

'*Quiet!*' warned Weavers.

'Without me, you don't have a hope in hell.'

'*Shut up, I said!*' yelled Weavers and, lunging forward, he slammed the butt of his gun hard into O'Brien's kidneys, making him sink to his knees.

Stepping back again, Weavers barked,

'Lew — go fetch some rope. We'll hog-tie him an' throw him in your cellar till Tom gets back. Gag 'im, too.'

O'Brien, feeling nauseous again, looked up at Glass, caught and held his frightened eyes. Glass stared back at him, his fair-to-red hair hanging loose across his sweaty forehead, his lips working soundlessly.

Speaking through his teeth, Weavers said, 'Get the rope, Lew.'

And like the sad, defeated little man that he was, Glass said, 'A-all right.'

He bent and picked up the fallen tumbler, went to put it back on the table beside his chair — then suddenly turned at the waist and hurled the glass at Weavers instead.

Startled, Weavers cried out and tried to dodge the missile, but he wasn't fast enough. It caught him a glancing blow on the forehead and he staggered, righted himself and fired his Colt, perhaps deliberately, perhaps by accident.

The slug slammed into the wall

behind Glass, but by then Glass, now acting out of pure, blind terror, had grabbed up the lamp and was charging across the room, a sound close to an Apache war-cry spitting from his mouth.

As shadows rose and fell on the walls, Weavers thumbed back for another shot, but before he could squeeze the trigger Glass smashed the lamp against the side of his head.

Weavers stumbled sideways, the right side of his face and shoulder suddenly covered in broken glass and warm kerosene. The kerosene ignited almost immediately and Weavers, screaming now, threw his gun aside and started beating at himself to put out the flames.

Glass staggered back, a look of horror stretching his pale face out of shape, and with no choice in the matter, O'Brien had to forget all about his own hurts and move fast. He clawed back to his feet, turned and punched the burning man square in the face, and Weavers bounced off the wall behind him and collapsed in a heap.

Suppressing a groan, O'Brien spun to the window, tore down the nearest drape and flung it over Weavers' head and shoulders to smother the flames. For a moment after that there was only the sound of their hard breathing.

Then O'Brien threw back the drape so they could examine Weavers' face by the meagre moonlight that filtered through the window. The right side looked red and blistered, the ear black and shrivelled, the man's fine dark hair burned down to the scalp. He'd live, O'Brien thought. But from this day forward, every time he looked in the mirror he'd see a wrinkled patchwork of scars, and remember just what his treachery had cost him.

Shoving back up, he said breathlessly, 'I'm . . . obliged, Lew. Looks like . . . you've got backbone after all.'

'I'm the same damn' coward I always was,' Glass grumbled ruefully. 'But I guess there's no turnin' back now, so . . . what's your plan?'

O'Brien clapped him on the arm. 'Go fetch the best saddle-horse you've got,' he said. 'I'll tell you on the way.'

★ ★ ★

As Circle G fell behind them, Glass told him all about the country up ahead — a vast plateau scored through with belts of sumac and cottonwood, snow-berry and Gambel oak, flanked by the San Juans to the south and good farming land to the north. Beautiful, well-watered country, he said, but a tough one through which to drive cattle. They'd slow Tom down, as would the chuck wagon and remuda he'd arranged to have waiting for him when he brought the herd out of the high country. 'So it should be easy enough to catch up with him, if that's what you've got in mind,' he finished.

'It's not,' O'Brien replied, wincing at his mount's every movement. 'Right now, Tom's doing the one thing Jane could never have done by herself

— getting the herd to White River. I'm not about to do anything to stop *that*.'

'So you figure to let Tom an' his boys do all the work for you,' Glass breathed, as understanding dawned at last.

'*And* wear themselves down in the process,' O'Brien confirmed.

For the next four days, then, they followed a route that paralleled the regular trail south and west, but never once came within sight of it. And though they deliberately held to a steady pace, the journey still took its toll and gave Glass serious cause for concern every time they quit for the day and he saw just how ragged O'Brien was becoming.

Luckily, they reached their destination around noon of the fifth day. They made camp in a stand of mountain mahogany about a quarter-mile away and Glass fixed a smokeless fire. Then, while their coffee boiled, he explained the layout of the place, having been there many times before.

The army had built a garrison on the

Agency's southernmost fringe, a wall-less scattering of squat log buildings centred around a dusty parade ground, reached from this side by a wide, sturdy bridge that spanned the slow-flowing river that gave the place its name. Further north lay the vast sprawl of the reservation itself, where most of the Ute nation had been given houses they didn't really want and taught to farm land that was nowhere near as good as the millions of acres the government had taken away from them a decade earlier.

He finished by pointing to a large house south of the parade ground, which he said were the quarters of White River's commanding officer, Major Edward Campbell, a conscientious, God-fearing man he knew reasonably well.

All they could do after that was watch and wait.

Around late afternoon two days later, Glass noticed a pall of dust in the sky to the north-east and said, 'Them?'

O'Brien, still too stiff and achy to

pose much of a threat to Tom and his men, took a look through the field-glasses and nodded. 'Them,' he replied.

At the head of the shuffling, strung-out column came Tom himself, slouched in the saddle of his smoke-grey gelding, his manner mean and challenging even at this distance. And behind him, making hard work of it because they weren't cowboys by trade, came his men, whistling or slapping bunched lariats against their legs, or waving their hats as they weaved through the dust of better than six hundred hoofs, determined to keep the animals moving.

The animals. Gaunted by the journey but still indisputably magnificent, they pushed on with their huge, shaggy heads held low between their massive shoulders, bellowing in protest at every weary step they took.

Then came the remuda, fifteen horses strong, being hazed along by the wrangler, a bandanna tied around his lower face to keep the dust out of his lungs. And about a hundred yards behind them came the chuck wagon, shivers running the length of its oft-repaired bonnet every time it rattled over a patch of especially rough ground.

O'Brien stiffened then, when he spotted Jane on the seat beside the lanky, sour-faced cook. She looked tired and lifeless, her hands in her lap, her shoulders slack, her eyes downcast, the odd strand of red hair hanging loose.

Moments later, the herd, the remuda and the wagon were all crossing the bridge, knocking trapped dust from between its sturdy planks to filter down into the water below, and all at once the garrison was a hive of activity, as soldiers came out to point and speculate, confused by critters that were neither cow nor buffalo, but a peculiar hybrid of the two.

With Tom seemingly everywhere at once, stabbing his one arm in every direction as he bawled orders in that gravel-laced voice of his, the cattalo were herded toward a sizeable corral to the north-east. Meanwhile, the chuck wagon and remuda headed for a timbered spot further north along the riverbank, where the wrangler strung up a rope corral for his horses and the cook set about fixing supper. Satisfied that all was as it should be Tom finally angled his horse across the parade ground and headed for Major Campbell's quarters.

For the rest of the day they kept watch on the garrison. Tom's men, eager for some comfort after the drive, washed up, ate a hasty supper and then headed for the sutler's store on the western edge of the parade ground. A while later, Tom left the CO's quarters, mounted up and rode over to join them.

Twilight came, blanketing the camp with purple shadows. Lights began to show at small, tarpaper windows all over the post, and enlisted men headed for the mess and their evening meal. At last O'Brien muttered, 'Time'.

They tightened girths and mounted up, crossed the bridge in the crimson light of sunset and walked their horses north, toward the Circle G chuck wagon. As they approached, O'Brien saw Jane sitting close to the wagon's left-side front wheel with her arms behind her, and it came to him in a sudden angry flare that she'd been tied there. The ribby-looking, dark-whiskered cook, meanwhile, was searching for some elusive object in back of the vehicle, clattering pots and pans as he did so.

Moments later Jane heard the sound of their horses and looked up, the small fire throwing lively shadows across her troubled face. At first she saw only a pair of riders she assumed were two of Tom's men. But then, as she looked closer and noticed something familiar about O'Brien's horse, about the width and shape of its rider's shoulders, her expression changed and she suddenly stiffened.

Before she could say anything, O'Brien silenced her with a quick gesture, and when they were near enough, he swung down and let his reins trail.

The cook, hearing them ride in, called out, 'That you, Tate?'

O'Brien went around to the back of the wagon and said, 'Nope.'

Startled by the unfamiliar voice, the cook turned with a rusty carving knife in one hand. O'Brien hit him twice, once in the stomach, one on the back of the head when he bent forward at the waist. The man fell unconscious at his feet.

He sucked in a breath, having jarred his ribs during the action, but forced the pain down and went back around the wagon, where Glass had also dismounted and was using a clasp-knife to cut through Jane's bonds.

She came to her feet, rubbing her wrists, animation coming back into her features. 'Mr O'Brien! What — ?'

'That can wait,' he replied, reaching out fast to stop her throwing herself at him. 'Just take my horse and go with Lew. He'll do all the talking.'

She frowned. 'What about you?'

'I've got business elsewhere.'

'Tom,' she said, her lips thinning.

There was no need to reply, so he just helped her to mount up. When she was safely in the saddle, she reached down impulsively and grabbed his hand. 'Thank you,' she whispered.

His lips quirked briefly. 'I said you weren't finished yet, didn't I?'

He watched the two of them walk their horses back toward the parade ground, headed for Campbell's quarters. Then the sounds of men letting off steam in the sutler's store drifted to him on the cool night breeze, and as his eyes turned that way, his expression hardened.

Flipping the restraining thong off the hammer of the Lightning, he started toward the sound of all that merriment.

The sutler's store was a sorry-looking log building with a pitched shingle roof and smeared windows through which lamplight glowed invitingly. As he came closer, he heard the exchange of bawdy comments and harsh laughter, the clink of whiskey bottle against glass, and then, almost before he knew it, he was there, at the door, pulling down one final, steadying breath, but still feeling like hell and knowing he was nowhere near up to the task he'd set himself.

He opened the door and went inside.

The store was hazy with cigarette smoke, and the stuffy air smelled of cheap booze and spices. It looked exactly like what it was — a store and a saloon all crammed into one. Tom and his gunnies, all travel-stained and whiskery, were bellied up to a plank-and-barrel bar that ran along the left-side wall, seemingly determined to drink the place dry. On the other side of the cigarette-burned plank floor stood a cracker-barrel and a coffee grinder, a counter topped with pilfer-proof glass and ceiling-high shelves stacked with everything from cut plug and long johns to spare lamps and canned sardines.

All eyes turned when O'Brien closed the door behind him and walked slowly into the centre of the room, and all at once there was no more banter, no more laughter, just a sudden, heavy, expectant silence.

Tom turned and put his back to the bar, and his companions followed suit. But if Tom was surprised to see him there, he certainly wasn't letting it show. His green, flint-hard eyes displayed only anticipation, and his nose wrinkled a little as the thin lips beneath it tugged into a wintry smile.

'Well, well,' he said.

O'Brien's only response was, 'It's over, Tom.'

Tom's grin widened. 'Is it, now?'

O'Brien nodded. 'By now, the army knows just how you got hold of Jane Farrow's herd. That it's not yours to sell.'

'An' you think the army'll take your word over mine?'

'No. But they'll take the word of Circle G's rightful owner.'

'Glass?' Tom rasped, suddenly stiffening. 'Glass'll never go again me.'

'He already *has*.'

'You're bluffin',' said Tom.

'I didn't come all this way to *bluff* you,' O'Brien returned quietly. 'I came to *finish* you.'

The silence was thick and cloying now, as every man there sifted the implications of what O'Brien had just said. If he was telling it true, if Lew Glass really *had* come to deny ownership of the herd, they were finished, the lot of them, because they still hanged cattle-thieves in these parts, and in the eyes of the law that's exactly what they were.

Down at the end of the makeshift bar, the sutler, a fat, bearded man in a stained chambray shirt, glanced nervously out the nearest window and stammered, 'I think you boys better git. They's soldiers comin'!'

Tom only sneered. 'What else do you expect? This place is *fulla* soldiers!'

Javier took a look out into the darkness. 'I see 'em. They're on the other side of the parade ground but they're comin' this way, an' they look like they mean business,' he reported. 'An' hell! Lew's with 'em! The Farrow woman, too!'

Tom made a dismissive sound in his throat and, as if it were no big deal, he said, 'Then we'll *give* 'em business. They make trouble, we'll *fight* our way out.'

'Take on the army?' Javier whispered, narrowing his eyes. 'The hell with that!' And he started toward the door, figuring to get the hell and gone while he still had the chance.

Almost too fast to see, Tom's left hand blurred across his narrow chest and came back filled with Army .44. He fired once and blew Javier's spine through his stomach.

The force of it slammed Javier forward, blood bursting out of his back in a red mist as he hit the floor like a sack of meat. Not waiting to see him fall, however, the one-armed man spun around to take O'Brien down as well — except that O'Brien was no longer there for the taking.

Seeing Tom's draw, knowing he couldn't beat it — certainly not in the shape he was in right then — he threw himself behind the counter, dropped to his knees with no thought for his tender ribs and tore the .38 from leather. In the store itself, meanwhile, pandemonium erupted as Tom's gunnies found themselves torn between shooting their way out or following Javier's example and trying to make a break for it.

Above all the chaos, Tom started screaming obscenities at the top of his voice, calling O'Brien every filthy son of a whore under the sun as he emptied his gun into the counter, splintering wood, shattering glass, driving lead through the cracker barrel and sending it whining off the coffee grinder.

O'Brien waited until he figured Tom's gun was empty, then came around the side of the cracker barrel, snap-aimed and fired at the last place he'd seen the one-armed man. But Tom, realizing himself that he needed to reload, was already racing for a doorway in the back wall of the store, and even as O'Brien tracked him, Tom put his shoulder to the door and smashed through it, splintering it off its hinges.

O'Brien broke cover and surged after him, just as another of Tom's men decided to leave by the front door. He heard yelling behind him, followed by a sudden rattle of gunfire and a shattering of glass, and told himself, *Yeah. The soldiers mean business, all right.*

The broken door opened into a kind of stockroom. Tom had deliberately spilled some packing cases on his way out and O'Brien stumbled over them in the dark but somehow kept going. A door at the far end of the room had been left ajar: beyond it, he saw a moon-washed yard, empty crates stacked at the far end, and beyond the low fence, the flickering lights of the camp infirmary and an inkier patch of darkness beside it that marked the position of the army graveyard.

He crashed out into the night, his

bruised chest complaining something fierce. Over the blood thundering in his ears, he heard a familiar, discordant rattling of spurs and turned just in time to see Tom disappear around the side of the building.

He dashed after him, blind to all else now save the desire to get this thing finished. But even as he reached the corner, he realized that he could no longer hear Tom's spurs, that Tom was no longer moving — that Tom hadn't gone any further than the corner.

In the next instant Tom loomed up right in front of him.

With a scream, the one-armed man lunged forward and brought his still-empty Colt down in a tight, savage arc. O'Brien hauled up just in time, back-pedalled to avoid the blow and, meeting no resistance, Tom stumbled forward but recovered fast. Turning sideways on, he came at O'Brien much as he'd gone at the storeroom door, and they met with a vicious slam of muscle against muscle and went spilling to the ground, O'Brien's Colt skittering off into the darkness.

Planting himself on O'Brien's chest, Tom brought his pistol up again, figuring to hammer his opponent's brains out, but O'Brien grabbed for the lapel of his All-Around duster and flung him sideways before he could do any such thing. Tom went over with a crash and a curse, recovered almost at once and brought his right leg up, then down on O'Brien's left shin, the spur ripping his flesh to the bone.

The pain was impossible to describe, almost more than he could stand, and while he tried to fight it down Tom leapt back to his feet, shoved the .44 under the stump of his right arm and set about reloading, muttering cuss-words all the while.

O'Brien rolled onto his side, left leg covered in blood, the icy pain already transforming into something infinitely more fiery. He heard more shouting coming from the sutler's store as Campbell's soldiers jammed inside and took the remaining gunnies prisoner.

Above him, Tom finished reloading, stabbed the Colt down at the back of O'Brien's head and snarled, '*This is for Al, you sonofabitch*!'

But just then another voice tore through the night. '*Drop it, Tom*!'

Tom spun as Lew Glass came heaving around the corner, unarmed and gasping for breath. He swore again and let Glass have the slug he'd intended for O'Brien, and Glass screamed, grabbed his right shoulder and fell.

With hardly a pause, he brought the gun back down and fired at O'Brien, but the shot was rushed and the bullet smacked into the ground beside him.

Self-preservation swamped the need for revenge, then. If Glass was here, the soldiers couldn't be far behind. So Tom pitched forward into a sprint, headed across the garrison towards his makeshift camp, the horses, and escape.

Deafened by the gunblasts, O'Brien rolled over, feeling closer to death than life. He shoved onto all fours, found his gun and limped to the overweight rancher. He was bleeding heavily now, and much as he didn't want to do it, every step brought a low sob from him. He dropped down beside Glass, croaked, 'Easy, Lew . . . '

'I'm . . . all right,' breathed Glass. 'Hurts like the devil, but . . . Ah, Christ, man! Wh-what's he done to you?'

It was a moment before O'Brien realized that Glass wasn't staring at his leg, but looking at his chest. He looked down himself and saw that his shirt was stained with a small rosette of blood. He hadn't been shot, so what . . . ?

One of his busted ribs had broken again and pushed through his skin.

A shudder went through him and he fought the urge to puke. He said, 'Hold on, Lew. Hold on.'

Then he grabbed the wall and dragged himself back to his feet, started crossing the compound in an old man's shuffle, the breath sawing in his throat. He felt giddy, his vision was blurring, and he wasn't sure he could make it.

'*Mr O'Brien!*'

And suddenly Jane was there, to his right, walking beside him. 'It's over,' she said, her voice high, excited. 'They've rounded up — ' She fell quiet then, as she looked from his face to his chest, from his chest to his leg. 'Oh, my God . . . ' she said, and started weeping.

He glanced at her, mumbled, 'Help me, Mrs F-Farrow. Tom — '

'*Forget* Tom! He'll kill you for sure if you go after him now!'

'Just get me over to the corral,' he said.

Knowing better than to argue with him, she did her best to lead him that way.

Already made nervous by all the gunfire, the cattalo were milling around the corral in agitated circles, heads down, a low, ominous bellow coming from several of them. And each beast's unease was slowly but surely communicating itself to the others, spreading like a contagion. The cattalo, once so docile and easy to move, were becoming ornery, their eyes small, hard and dangerous as they watched O'Brien and Jane come closer.

But O'Brien could hear another sound now, the throbbing beat of horse-hoofs moving at speed, and he thought he knew what that meant.

He took his arm from Jane's shoulders and told her to find cover. She opened her mouth, shook her head, but one look at his fevered face told her to do as he said. Lifting her skirts she backed a few yards away from him, watching as he reached the corral gate, then turned and leaned heavily against the rails, worn down, worn *out*, wanting nothing better than to collapse and let the rest of the world take care of itself, but knowing there was still one last job to do.

A rider burst out of the trees away to his right, hunched low over his horse's flying mane.

Tom.

O'Brien watched him come, in focus one minute, out of it the next. There was no way he could hope to hit him now, not in this light, at this distance, in this condition. But if he was lucky he wouldn't have to.

As the one-armed man drew level with him, no more than thirty, forty yards away, he yelled, '*Tom!*'

Grandee glanced to his left, saw O'Brien standing — if you could call it standing — in front of the corral and hauled back on the reins to bring the horse to a messy halt.

'*Running out on me, Tom?*' O'Brien bawled. '*Is that it?*'

'*There'll be another time!*' yelled Tom.

O'Brien appeared to consider that, as Tom gathered his reins and prepared to ride on. But then he called back, '*Guess Al didn't mean that much to you after all, huh?*'

That did it. *Al.* And as he heard O'Brien yell his brother's name, Tom's fury came boiling back to the surface and all common sense deserted him. He reached across his thin body for the Colt, tore it free and then started galloping towards him, shouting something, bringing his arm up before him, taking aim —

O'Brien raised the Lightning and fired two shots. They tore up the ground directly in front of the charging horse, made it to break stride, rise up onto its hind legs and start flailing at the air, and Tom, caught off-balance, fell backwards out of the saddle to smash hard against the packed dirt of the parade ground.

The horse came down on all fours, scared senseless and showing it. Lifting its head high to keep from stumbling on its trailing reins, it began to run back the way it had just come.

Undaunted, Tom powered back to his feet, spit-flecked curses dropping from his contorted mouth as he thrust the .44 ahead of him again and started stagger-running toward O'Brien, firing as he did so.

O'Brien, somehow managing to stand his ground, reached for the gate behind him, wrenched it open and thought, *Come and get it, you sonofabitch.*

He emptied his gun into the air, shot after shot after shot, then stumbled sideways into Jane's arms just as the spooked *cattalo* surged forward and out through the gate. One, three, five, nine, a dozen, more, more, each one a relentless, inescapable juggernaut, moving at a rate of speed that belied its awesome size.

Tom saw them pour from the corral, spread wide and race toward him. He saw the size of them, the *number* of them, the unstoppable, rumbling speed of them, and they filled his ears with thunder, blocked his nose and scratched his eyes with dust, and made the ground shake beneath his feet.

O'Brien saw his eyes go wide, saw that familiar hard, flat, never-give-an-inch hatred in them, and then he saw something he never thought he'd ever see — fear.

Tom emptied his gun into the

charging herd but did no damage, then vanished from sight as the cattalo tore him off his feet, shattered his bones and pulped his flesh, stamped and crushed him until all that was left was just a red, jellied smear.

Tom was gone, and it was over. O'Brien lasted just long enough to see that for himself. Then his eyes rolled up into his head and he collapsed. He didn't hear Jane scream his name. He didn't hear *anything*. And he didn't move again.

★ ★ ★

Half the garrison turned out when all hell broke loose, and enlisted men, most of whom had never worked cattle before, much less *cattalo*, were soon put to work rounding up the scattered herd. Tom's men — those who survived the brief shoot-out at the sutler's store — were placed under arrest until a federal marshal could be called in and charges brought.

O'Brien died on the parade ground and went to Heaven, or leastways that's how it seemed to him. For quite a time there was no more pain and no more violence, just a place of peace and quiet where he could rest and recover.

When he finally regained consciousness around the middle of the following afternoon, he realized that *Heaven* was actually the camp infirmary, where his assorted injuries had been tended and, with any luck, would finally be given the chance to heal properly.

Jane was sitting beside the narrow cot when he woke up. It was a bright, blue-sky day and the infirmary was filled with sunshine. Dimly it occurred to him that it was a good day to be alive.

'Here,' said Jane, immediately starting to fuss over him, 'let me get you some water.'

He drank, put his head back on the pillow. 'Are you all right?' he asked.

'I'm fine. Everything's fine, now. Lew Glass has been a tower of strength.'

O'Brien frowned. 'He's OK?'

'Tom shot him in the arm, and he lost a lot of blood, but the army surgeon says he'll be all right.' She shook her head in wonder. 'You know, I never thought he had it in him, but he gave Major Campbell a full account of how Tom took the herd. He took care of everything.'

'He's a good man,' O'Brien told her. 'I owe him *my* life.' Then his frown came back. 'What about the herd?'

Jane said, 'The army's more than happy with its purchase, now it's gotten over the surprise of seeing exactly what Tom brought them,' she said. 'The buffalo means a lot to the Utes, as you doubtless know. Major Campbell believes they'll see the *cattalo* as being equally special.'

'They're special, all right,' he allowed. 'I'm glad it all worked out, Mrs Farrow.'

'So am I,' she said, but suddenly her face shadowed again. 'And yet so much hate, so much pain, so much death. Was it all worth it?'

'You did what you had to do. You turned your husband's dream into a reality. Was *that* worth it?'

'Of course. But Abel — '

'Abel wanted you folks to look after yourselves. And that's what you've got to do.'

'There's something else I have to do, too,' she said. 'And that's look after *you*. At least until you're back on your feet.'

'Don't worry about me, Mrs Farrow. I heal fast.'

'Not *too* fast, I hope,' she cautioned, the beginnings of a smile touching her full lips again. 'I'm looking forward to nursing you back to health, Mr O'Brien. And I think Clay will enjoy having you around for a while, too. So no arguments, you hear me?'

'Ma'am,' O'Brien said, and meant it, 'I never argue with a woman who wants to treat me like a hero.'

We do hope that you have enjoyed reading this large print book.

Did you know that all of our titles are available for purchase?

We publish a wide range of high quality large print books including:
Romances, Mysteries, Classics
General Fiction
Non Fiction and Westerns

Special interest titles available in large print are:
The Little Oxford Dictionary
Music Book, Song Book
Hymn Book, Service Book

Also available from us courtesy of Oxford University Press:
Young Readers' Dictionary
(large print edition)
Young Readers' Thesaurus
(large print edition)

For further information or a free brochure, please contact us at:
Ulverscroft Large Print Books Ltd.,
The Green, Bradgate Road, Anstey,
Leicester, LE7 7FU, England.
Tel: (00 44) **0116 236 4325**
Fax: (00 44) **0116 234 0205**

CARSON'S REVENGE

Jim Wilson

When the Mexican bandit General Rodriguez hangs Carson's grandfather, the youngster vows revenge, and with that aim joins the Texas Rangers. Then as Carson escorts Mexican Henrietta Xavier to her home, Rodriguez kidnaps her. The ranger plucks the heiress from the general's clutches, and the youngsters make a desperate run for the border and safety. Will Carson's strength and courage be enough to save them as he tries to get the better of the brutal general and his bandits?